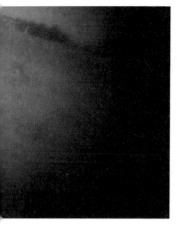

D0398966

Rosie
A Dainty Companion
We love You
R.I.P

REC'D JUN 03 2019

THE NIGHT SWIMMERS

Also by the author

SPELLS
Klickitat
The Shelter Cycle
My Abandonment
The Unsettling
The Bewildered
The Ambidextrist
Carnival Wolves
This Is the Place

THE NIGHT SWIMMERS

—

Peter Rock

Published by
Soho Press Inc.
853 Broadway
New York, NY 10003

Library of Congress Cataloging-in-Publication Data

Rock, Peter, 1967–
The night swimmers / Peter Rock.

ISBN 978-1-64129-000-5
eISBN 978-1-64129-001-2

I. Title.
PS3568.O327 N54 2019 813'.54—dc23 2018040582

Interior design by Janine Agro, Soho Press, Inc.

Printed in the United States of America

10 9 8 7 6 5 4 3 2 1

THE NIGHT
SWIMMERS

ONE

- 1 -

To swim with another person—out in the open water at night, across a distance, without stopping—is like taking a walk without the pressure, the weight of having to carry a conversation, to bring what is inside to the outside. Think of being with someone in a silent room, the tension in the air; water is thicker and you can't talk, can't stop moving. Instead, you're together, struggling along, only glimpsing each other's silhouetted arm or head for a moment, when you turn your face to breathe, a reassurance that you are not completely alone.

I remember the straight black line of Mrs. Abel's clavicle, her shadow on the road that summer, overlapping mine. Her collar hanging open, another time, her thin hand on the toaster—pushing down the lever, then her palm hovering there, feeling the heat. The low whisper of her voice, her stories of shipwrecks in Death's Door, the floor of the lake like the forest floor, bones and timbers collapsing, scattered by the currents.

I remember Mrs. Abel's slender arms—one, then the

other—bent above the surface of the water, her face flashing in the moonlight. We swam through the darkness, parallel, rising and falling across the black swells. Ahead, the distant silhouette of the tower. Headlights winked through the trees, cars driving on the road atop the bluff. I breathed to my right, she to her left, checking for each other. Below us, depths.

- 2 -

The night of Mrs. Abel's party, I walked down out of the cedars, onto the white stones of the beach. A storm was coming in, rows of whitecaps tearing across the lake, the wind gusting cold. I started along the shoreline, almost tripping over the taut ropes that stretched from the trees to the rowboats and canoes that were pulled up beyond the waves' reach.

It was June of 1994, and I was twenty-six. I'd returned from various wanderings to live again with my parents, and was maintaining vague dreams of becoming a writer, of writing. My parents were alternately patient and impatient with this; they told me that I could stay for the summer, on that thin peninsula in Wisconsin where I'd spent every summer of my boyhood. I was secretly planning to stay through the autumn, as long as I could before the winter drove me away. I had nowhere else to go, nowhere I was supposed to be.

The wind rattled the metal fittings of the flagpole, out on the end of Zimdars' dock. As I headed down the beach, under the lights of our neighbors' houses, I felt the temptation with each dock and pier I passed, the desire to shed my clothes and run to the end, to leap off into the dark waves. I loved to swim, and I loved to swim at night.

A few nights before, I'd been out swimming along this shoreline and I'd seen flickering lights, shifting shadows in the windows of the rundown cabin set near where our road dead-ended, a house that had long been dark. All the people along the shore were equally surprised to hear that the cabin was inhabited. Few had known Mr. Abel well, nor had anyone seen him in quite some time; few had even known that he had passed away, and no one was aware that he'd recently been married. The invitations to the party had come from the old man's widow.

Like everyone else, I was curious, drawn by the mystery. I myself hadn't exactly been invited to the party—my parents had been, though my father chose not to go. My excuse was that I was going to retrieve my mother, walk her home through the darkness.

Once I reached the Abel cabin, I paused, standing below it, on the beach. I could hear voices from the party, laughter. In the lit windows above I could see the heads, the upper bodies of people I knew—the Hoags, the Glenns—and then some I didn't know, one of whom was likely Mrs. Abel.

I stepped into the trees, out of the moonlight, past the wooden doors that closed off the storage space beneath the Abel cabin. I climbed the slope around the cabin, toward the back door, which was open. People were leaving and, exuberant with wine, they shouted my name when they saw me.

"You're all grown up!"

"Getting any writing done?"

"Thinking about that day job, yet?"

I joked along, uneasily, making my way through the door, into the dim cabin. I was used to this banter; the uneven, sporadic way I'd see these people—only in the summer, often years apart—was a syncopation that brought wonder at my growth, when I was young, and had now degenerated into a kind of embarrassment at my stasis, my stalled progress.

Inside, the cabin was lit by candles, two kerosene lanterns on a table; shadows flickered along the walls. Bowls full of different colored beach glass—blue, white, and green—caught the candle-light from atop a piano. The cabin was small, shaped like an L. I didn't see my mother; most of the voices and people seemed to be around the corner, in what must have been the kitchen.

I crossed the shadowy room, past a low, threadbare couch, around a table. One window faced the lake, and beside it a wooden ladder slanted, leading to a sleeping loft above. The ladder had been sawn off, ten feet up, and was splattered with white paint. Reaching out, I touched one of its rungs, the duct tape wrapped around it.

People behind me were talking about the old man. When and how he'd died, who had seen him last. Lakeside property—who had it, who might sell or inherit it, taxes—was a favorite topic up and down the shore. Some at the party had no doubt been maintaining designs on this cabin, this parcel of land, and so they were curious where this mysterious widow had come from, and how she came to possess this property, what were her intentions.

The air in the room smelled like kerosene, sharp and acrid, tight in my throat. The sound of the wind and the waves came through the window next to me, rattled the glass. Next to the window, a piece of paper had been set with one nail into the log wall; one side was torn, its edge like the lip of a wave—it had been torn from a book, and candlelight flickered along the image. It was a painting of a fire in a spare forest, red leaves or sparks leaping above the flames, into the broken branches of the charred trees above. The moon shone down, and in the background, at the bottom of a slope, stood a small cabin, striped white and gray—concrete and timber, just like the one I was standing inside. The yellow window of that cabin could be the one I was standing beside. Suddenly I felt trapped, claustrophobic; I closed my eyes, certain that if I looked out the window I would see a forest fire in the moonlight rather than the storm coming across the lake.

"Are you going to climb into my bedroom?"

I let loose of the ladder and turned to face her, this woman whom I'd never seen before, who had to be Mrs. Abel. She was tall and slender, as tall as I was, almost six feet.

"No," I said. "I just—"

"You can, if you want," she said, gesturing at the loft. "Go ahead."

"I just came for my mother," I said, glancing past Mrs. Abel, toward the kitchen. "To walk her home."

"I know who you are," she said. "You're the swimmer."

We were alone in the room, and it was uncomfortable; it felt impolite to look straight at her, but I could see that she wore pale blue moccasins, the kind with beads on top, black and white and red in the shape of a bird. No socks, her ankles exposed, her khakis reaching halfway to her calves. Her shirt was a blue Oxford with the sleeves rolled up, its tail long—perhaps it had belonged to her husband—and its collar threadbare. She lifted her hand, adjusted her braid, and I saw the pale flash of her neck, the nape, for an instant. Smiling, she looked at me, her eyes at the same level as mine. Pale eyes, blue, her bangs cut straight, just above them; her black hair was shot through with strands of gray.

"Isn't that true?" she said.

"What?"

"That you're the swimmer."

"I guess," I said. "I like to swim."

"How far do you go?" she said.

"I don't know. As far as I can. Went out to Horseshoe the other day."

That was the closest island, just over two miles from our shore.

Turning away, I leaned close to the window so I could see past my reflection, out to the black waves rolling across the lake. I couldn't see the silhouette of the distant island.

"I love storms," Mrs. Abel said. "Don't you?"

In that moment, she drew closer. I felt as if she was going to reach out and touch me, but she did not.

"Your mother left half an hour ago," she said, her voice a whisper. "Before you got here. She must not have known you were coming."

"I came along the beach," I said. "I guess she came through the woods, or the road."

People emerged from the kitchen, then, waving and saying goodnight, saying thank you as they stood in the doorway. The party was coming to an end.

"Nice to talk with you, swimmer," Mrs. Abel said, and went to say her goodbyes.

I slipped around the group of people, slipped away from the cabin; I hurried down the slope, out of the trees, to the beach, back the way I'd come.

The storm was still rising, the waves higher, crashing to cover the sound of my breathing, of my feet on the stones that glowed white beneath the moon. When I reached our cabin, I saw that the waves had knocked our canoe and rowboat from their wooden ramps, had turned them sideways. I pulled the boats—the rowboat heavier, its square stern filled with water—further up under the trees, beyond the water's reach.

I climbed one of the cedars, thirty or forty feet up until I was near the top and my weight added to the wild sway brought by the gusting wind. The tree rattled its branches against the other trees close around it. I held on, watching our raft tilt and spin, twenty yards from shore as the waves lifted it, passing beneath. Long rows of whitecaps swept across the lake, lightning on the horizon—it made me feel that something was changing, finally beginning. I held on at the top of the cedar as the storm rose, as it arrived. A mile and a half away, across the waves, the moon shone on the white face of Eagle Bluff. Closer, the waves crashed into and slapped over the thin wooden pier that jutted like a splintery finger from our shore. And then a gust of wind picked up the beach chairs and cartwheeled them along the stones.

- 3 -

Mrs. Abel told me once that the party was an attempt to handle all the introductions at once, and to lessen people's interest in and curiosity about her. In this latter desire, she failed. The peninsula in the summer was a place of leisure, of talk, and the gossip was drawn to what was unknown, what could be speculated upon, this natural mystery brought among us. People described Mrs. Abel as "striking," a "striking woman," which always felt to me like an aggressive way to say it. Her blue eyes—I heard people describe them as "piercing," as if they might stab right through you.

She speaks many languages—English isn't even her first.
She doesn't own a car, she doesn't talk small talk.
She washes her clothing in the lake.
She's a severe vegetarian.
She was married to him for less than a month before he died.
She tore out all the electrical wiring in her cabin.

Someone reported seeing Mrs. Abel running along the highway at night, her shoes in her hands and her hair loose in her face. Others said that Mr. Abel was not her first husband, and quite possibly not even her second. Some wives felt that Mrs. Abel was over-friendly with their husbands; others claimed she was equally unfriendly to everyone; still others suggested that she was shy, quiet. And she was grieving, after all.

There was the talk and then the talk under the talk, pulling everyone in, early that summer. An undertow—all childhoods are haunted by reports of this current, that takes hold of your feet and holds you under, that only lets loose once you've drowned. It is not a thing that can be suspected, let alone resisted (I think of Poe's "A Descent into the Maelstrom": "A bear once, attempting to swim from Lofoden to Moskoe, was caught by the stream and borne down, while he roared terribly, so as to be heard on shore. Large stacks of firs and pine trees, after being absorbed by the current, rise again broken and torn to such a degree as if bristles grew upon them.").

Books and experts claim that such vortices and currents don't actually exist, that they are exaggerations born of people trying to swim against a riptide—and yet, as I swim along the surface, I feel unseen weather, underwater winds.

Just the other morning, here in Oregon over twenty years later, I was walking my daughter to kindergarten. We were holding hands, talking about *The Long Winter*, which I'd been reading to her and her sister the night before.

"Do you think," she said, "that Laura should have married Cap Garland instead of Alonzo?"

"Definitely," I said.

"Would you marry Cap Garland?"

"Of course. If he asked."

"Why?"

"His name's cooler," I said, "for one thing. And Alonzo seemed kind of old."

Dropping my hand, she bent her head back; she looked up into the sky and said, "Those birds are flying in the shape of a question mark."

To me, it looked like a ragged, uncoiling spiral, disappearing over the brick elementary school, the treetops.

"Why do you think they're flying in that shape?" I asked her.

"They have a question up there," she said.

We walked on, past the balance beam and slide, the jungle gym, past older kids playing basketball.

"You can go, Daddy," she said, letting go of my hand.

"I'll stay with you," I said. "The bell hasn't rung, yet."

"I don't need you to stay," she said.

"I know that. Still—"

"I don't want you to," she said, and hurried away, past the bike rack; she looked up at the sky once more, then disappeared around the red brick building.

I followed, at a distance. I peered around the corner and saw her walk among the crowds of children and parents, not pausing or looking at anyone. Her face was so serious, self-sufficient and mysterious to me. She was prepared for the business of her day.

- 4 -

Two nights after the party, the rain, the thunder and lightning had passed. The thick black waves were still rolling in; I only had to fight through the first twenty yards or so—through the breakers in the shallows—and then I would swim parallel to the shoreline, along the swells and not against them. I'd rise on the crests and drop down into the troughs, breathing only to the onshore side and blind, as a consequence, to any rogue wave spiking up behind me.

Once I made it through the breakers, past the raft, I turned and looked back toward shore. From there I could see the lighted windows of our small cabin, the silhouettes of my parents, sitting up in their chairs, reading, and the windows of our neighbors' houses. And when I was out a little further, I could see the lights of the houses up on the bluff, above the road, above the tops of our trees.

I set out toward the town of Ephraim, south, a mile away, where I'd pass through the empty moored boats—their bows all pointed in the same direction, anchor lines angling down, masts black against the night sky—and see the lights of the Moravian church's sharp steeple, up on the hill. The lights of our shore, the houses, flashed when I turned my head to breathe. The Reeves, the Hoblers, Shattucks' abandoned dock, and then my grandparents' house and their old white-and-red metal speedboat, pulled up on shore.

Just the other night I dreamed I was supposed to sink that old red boat, to fill it with stones and take it out deep, to punch holes in the bottom and then let it slip away beneath me as I swam away. I worried that the boat would pull me down, too, that I'd be caught in the vacuum of its descent. And yet when I arrived at my grandparents' house, when I began to prepare myself, I was told that a dead body had been found on the beach, near the boat. I was told that no one should look at it, that it was something no one would want to see, to have caught in their memories. In fact, no one was allowed to go down to the beach at all. Nothing could be disturbed, as the authorities were coming to gather evidence, which meant that eventually they would take the body away. Only then could I sink the red boat, which is a responsibility I never fulfilled, as the dream ended and I awakened while still waiting for the authorities to arrive.

Swimming at night: to compare its slipperiness to that of a dream would be to ignore the work of staying afloat, the mesmerism brought on by the rhythm, the repetition of the strokes. That night, I passed Peterson's Point, fingertips brushing the rocky bottom in the shallows, then out into the blacker depths.

I felt in that moment the possibility that I was upside down, and the air had gone thick, the water thin, that I was suspended somehow over the blackness of the sky.

True, I knew the lakebed I swam across, its features and secrets, yet I did not know what the black water between it and the surface where I swam, what those currents held. The surface currents pushed and pulled me, they kept me from swimming a straight line, the currents of the Great Lakes subtler and quietly more sinister than those of the ocean, hardly whispering as they attempted to pull me astray. I could not be pulled astray; I had no investment in my destination. I only wanted to be out there in that weather, playing along, knowing that rip currents would pull a swimmer away from shore and that it was always a mistake to swim against them, to panic, to exhaust oneself. You must swim with a rip current, for a time, swim across and learn from it, to be patient and aware, also, that the currents of the subsurface are likely to be moving in different directions, at different speeds.

That is what is known as an undercurrent, that black space beneath me where sometimes I believed I saw faces staring up at me, sliding away as I swam across their ceiling.

Currents startled each other, collided beneath my body, merged into a kind of conversation, and I imagined all the lost drowned bodies, worn down by currents, nibbled by fish caught in the weather of that deep water, of that zone between top and bottom. That's where they often reside, the dead, sliding through the currents—they don't necessarily sink to the bottom or rise to the top, and I swam over those bodies, those skeletons, some incomplete, bones barely held together by tendons, bones rattling slowly as they swam through that darkness with newer bodies, cartwheeling beneath me in slow motion, skin covered in white fungus.

My eyes open that night, staring down, I could not know what would happen that summer—a foresight as impossible as seeing that a man my family knew would park behind our cabin, ten years later, and drown himself off a neighbor's dock. I simply kept swimming, maintaining my rhythm, cutting across the swells, the breathing of crest and trough, the rise and fall of the lake.

As I swam, I envisioned the hidden lake floor, somewhere beneath me, and my mind drifted to those tiny underwater castles in aquariums and fishbowls, the toy Poseidons with their miniature tridents, and to Sea Monkeys, which I'd once admired from the back of a comic book, convinced by the pink anthropoid family in the drawings—the leggy mother with the three-pronged head and upswept hair, the proud father with his tail covering his genitals, their underwater castle in the background (taken in also by the promise, *So eager to please, they can even be trained*, despite the fine print: *Caricatures shown not intended to depict artemia salina.*). I emptied the envelopes into water, I must have been seven or eight, and waited for the eggs to hatch; when they did, I gazed at the winged specks, hoping to differentiate and name them, finally setting the bowl on our piano, on the wooden cover that folded down above the keys. Later that afternoon, my older sister—in a rush to bang out "Toreador" or "The Entertainer" with ridiculous speed—jerked that cover open and spilled the bowl down into the keys. In time, we joked that we could hear the Sea Monkeys scream or sing along when the piano was played.

They were only brine shrimp, my sister pointed out, and that is true, that's all they were. Years later, I would stand up to my knees in the Great Salt Lake—the water there so salty a person cannot sink—with the woman who would become my wife. We bent down and squinted against the glare to see those winged specks, flitting and hovering above our bare feet. This was close to the Spiral Jetty, about which I once wrote a failed novel—that strange twisting rubble was underwater for all my childhood, a dark shadow visible only from a height, from a plane flying overhead. Fifteen hundred feet, fifteen feet wide, I've waded the length of the Jetty, around and around to its center. It is a vortex, a dimensional tornado that can take a person from one world into another, from one time to another time.

When I surfaced that night, when I stopped swimming long enough to rest, to look around myself, I found that I'd swum a long curve, a spiral away from shore and north instead of south. Instead of being near Ephraim, I was off the shore of Little Sister Bay, where the lighted windows revealed the shapes of houses, helping me recognize them. I swam in, closer, the water up to my chest as my feet found the rocky bottom.

The house nearest to me, shaped like the prow of a ship, all glass windows, belonged to the grandfather of an ex-girlfriend of mine. An old man with a gray beard and a temper—I'd once seen him back his station wagon over a neighbor boy's bike, then get out cursing and throw the broken bike deep into the forest. It was said that years ago, at the beginning of the twentieth century, he'd courted my grandmother, but that relationship hadn't taken, perhaps because of his wildness. His granddaughter had a Norwegian name that meant "quietly peaceful," which was not always perfectly aligned with my experience of her. By the night I paused there, offshore, a few years had passed; she may have already been married to a French tennis player, had a child. Was she inside, that night, as I watched? I could see shapes, shadows, but they were not for me. I had been in those rooms, done all manner and felt all manner of things, in those spaces, but it was no longer a place for me; there were no people there for me.

I turned back to the lake and began to swim, keeping the shoreline to my left, back toward home.

Even out in the open water, the waves had slackened, eased. The last energy of the storm tapering away. I swam.

Almost home, a shape caught my eye, a sharp black movement—a wing, a knife, off to the left when I turned my head to breathe, following me along. I stopped, lifted my head, treading water.

It was another swimmer, swimming parallel to me, thirty feet away, closer to shore. We swam along again, and when the other swimmer veered away, angling toward shore, I paused again, and watched.

The figure swam in long smooth strokes, slender arms and sharp hands, and disappeared—lost beneath the surface—for a moment before appearing again, slowing, a round head cutting the flat water in front of the thin, rickety pier in front of the Abel cabin.

It was Mrs. Abel, and I was twenty feet away in the waves, watching as she pulled herself up onto the pier, a thin silhouette against the white of the stones, the gray of the trees. She pulled off a swim cap, wrung water from her long hair. Turning, she looked out at the lake, toward me. Could she see me? Silently,

I glided closer, keeping my eyes on her, standing there. I was twenty feet away when she spoke.

"You're a night swimmer, too."

The moon shone down, the tops of the trees glowing behind and above her. Was she wearing a swimsuit? I couldn't tell. I didn't know what to say, my voice caught up.

"There aren't too many of us," she said.

Before I could respond, she turned and walked away down the pier. Her figure blended into the shadows beneath the trees.

I waited, for a moment, uncertain whether to follow or what to do. Finally, I swam back along the shore, toward home.

- 5 -

I didn't sleep in my parents' cabin; instead, I stayed in a shack up the slope, hidden in the woods. It had been built on the shore, a beach house where people changed clothes, and at some point it had been put on rollers, dragged up into the trees. Painted the red of a faded barn, it was named the Red Cabin, though it was more of a shack, with no running water. Ten by fifteen feet, one room, a slanted roof; its five square windows, all along one wall, were offset so they looked like a jagged row of teeth. The screen door's spring shrieked, and no one ever rung the metal bell on the wall outside, its clapper and mouth all ensnarled with cobwebs.

After swimming, I would walk through the woods to the Red Cabin. I'd come in to the sound of that screen door and the air was always moist, the damp smell of the straw mats on the floor, and I'd lay down on the futon that took up half the space. I'd turn over and look up at the orange-and-red Sunfish sail wrapped around its mast, various ropes hanging down, the black windsurfer booms casting wishbone shadows until I switched off the lamp. Before I fell asleep I wondered what would happen to me, and I wondered about Mrs. Abel, and I had no way of knowing.

And then sometimes I'd sit down at my little table, my hair still damp, and try to write. I had one small gooseneck lamp and in the window I could see my reflection, sitting there with a pen in my hand. I could also see through the window, up to the gravel road, where neighbors walked by in the dusk, where cars passed. I liked the feeling of sitting there, illuminated in the window. Any neighbor walking by could see me, there in that shack in the woods, pen in hand. They might comment on it, mention it to each other, to my parents, and would remember how I looked, sitting there, apparently deep in thought, writing.

Around that time, that summer, I remember telling someone that I wanted every story I wrote to say this, implicitly, to the reader:

I'm coming over to your house.

I thought that was an impressive thing to say, and I said it to impress this person, this young woman; in truth, I think I also believed it, that this kind of insistence was something to desire, a necessity.

Now, over twenty years later, my declaration has changed:

Will you please come along with me? I would like company. I'm uncertain where I'm going and I'm a little frightened.

I was sitting there at my red table in the Red Cabin, one night shortly after I'd seen Mrs. Abel swimming, and suddenly there she was, up on the road, walking past.

My knees jolted the underside of the table as I stumbled to my feet; I opened the door slowly, so it wouldn't shriek too loudly, and rushed out under the trees, after her.

Instead of going up to the road, I stayed in the woods, running parallel, keeping her silhouette in sight. She wasn't moving too fast, and as she walked she was singing; I moved closer, to hear, and realized it wasn't words, but only sounds, a melody.

I kept following, and then I sped up and got ahead—crossing the gravel driveway of my grandparents' house, then the Glenns'—before coming out of the bushes and heading back the way I'd come, so it would seem I was walking home along the road.

The moon was out, but the trees were tall and there were no streetlights. It was difficult to see faces.

"Is that you?" she said.

"You're out walking," I said, immediately embarrassed at the obviousness of this statement.

"Should I be sleeping?" she said. "Walking comes easier for me."

"Sometimes I can't sleep," I said.

We were silent for a moment, standing there awkwardly on the road, and then headlights swept around the bend, ratcheting through the trees. Anne Hobler, her white hair visible for a moment, cruised past in her old maroon sedan.

"I saw you," Mrs. Abel said, "I saw you sitting there in the window of your little cabin, and then all of a sudden you're here, coming from the other direction. Or was that someone else?"

"No."

"Or maybe there are two of you?"

We stood there in the moonlight, the sharp shadows of the trees on the blacktop. She was teasing me, and it was a different way of talking, a different tone than other adults used with me. She was an adult, but she wasn't as old as my parents; still, she was twice as old as I was.

"And so you rushed out here to intercept me," she said, "so our meeting would seem like a coincidence—"

"I don't know," I said. "I guess—"

"What were you doing," Mrs. Abel said, "sitting there in your cabin?"

"Writing," I said.

"Writing what?"

"Stories, I guess."

"How impractical!" she said, laughing.

"Well," I said. "I'm not writing much, anyway."

"I like that it's impractical." I could hear her smile in the darkness. "And what are these stories about?"

"I don't know," I said.

"Adventure stories? Love stories?"

"I guess I don't know what they'll be until I write them."

"You're so serious," she said. "I'm just giving you a hard time."

The moon cast shadows of the tall cedars on the road; the wind gusted and the dark shapes leapt and slid around us.

"I saw you swimming," I said.

"I've seen you, too," she said.

"I know," I said.

"Have you ever swum with another person?"

"Yes," I said. "Of course."

"At night, I mean. Distances. It's different."

As I thought of what to say, how to respond, she was already walking away from me. I was uncertain if I was supposed to follow, or if what she'd said was an invitation.

- 6 -

Near the end of his life, my grandfather wrote:

> *As I grow older, I dream much more. Usually including problems I have difficulty solving during my dream—then, during waking hours, I continue to try to solve them. Last night, I tried to change a fuse in a house we once lived in, now with a very complicated subterranean basement full of sparkling, involved fixtures. Couldn't find a flashlight or understand the circuit breaker. When I woke up, I went out to check if the flashlight was in its usual place.*

My grandfather excerpted his lifelong journals, his thoughts and musings, and made many copies of this manuscript, one of which he gave to me. He called it *The Hollow Tree* ("A Repository for my Acorns"), and in the preface he says that it is "meant primarily for my daughters, but also to help my memory retain thoughts by mortaring them in."

- 7 -

That night on the road, I didn't answer Mrs. Abel. I didn't follow her. I watched her walk away, disappear into the shadows.

I stepped off the road, into the woods, the trees, turning back the way I'd come. I started along paths I've known my whole life, and even in that darkness I knew the ground underfoot was the dark brown of dried cedar and around me the velvety leaves of sumac's new branches, the darkness of their red cones and the prickly bushes crowding the path, bright green in daylight, bright orange when the branches were dead. Here in the darkness I followed the paths of Horse Hideout—the white rocks, speckled with black, glowing against the night, those stones carefully stacked by my mother and her sisters, in their childhood, almost fifty years before.

I didn't return to the Red Cabin that night. Instead, I crossed the road and started along beneath the bluff, limestone cliffs that stretched over a mile, parallel to the shore—at one time they had been the shore, the lake stretching hundreds of feet higher. All these trees, the cliffs and the caves, all of this was underwater; I pretended I was able to breathe that dark water as I walked along the lake bed, looking for the path that slanted up the cliff so I could eventually surface.

The wide path was not easy to find; finally, I found the opening in the underbrush and headed upward. My mother wrote a poem about this path, about the past, and it hangs in the kitchen of our cabin (never happy with it, she's always asking me to critique it, then taking the frame apart and inserting new versions, new words):

One hundred years ago Anton Amundsen's
Cows ambled down the stony path above our road.
Shadowing the side of the cliff,
Tails flyflicking, udders swaying,
They quickened their pace and headed toward the Bay
Stone stepping the beach,
They lowered their heads and drank.

That night I swam up the path through those ghost cows, and near the top saw the yellow light, cast from the screen porch of the Zahn house, right at the edge of the cliff. Old Mr. Zahn was a widower and lived there alone, keeping to himself. He was sitting on his screen porch, twenty feet away as I passed. I knew he must see me; I waved and said hello, so he would know who it was.

He didn't wave back. His hands were in his lap—one held a knife, the other a piece of wood. His beard was white and suspenders red, his face so wrinkled I couldn't tell if his eyes were open or closed. He had fallen asleep.

I kept on, into an open field. Mr. Zahn had cut back the trees below (not appreciated by the neighbors who owned them) so he'd have a view of the lake, which was calm now, flat and dull in the moonlight. I could also see the tops of the houses below. The closest was Mrs. Abel's, empty now; she was somewhere else, walking by herself, further and further away from me.

Out in the woods I'd find skeletons of bleached bones. All the bones of an animal—if the deer or raccoon had collapsed, there—all its muscles and sinews gone loose and rotted, eaten away, fur gathered by birds and mice for nests, rolled across the forest floor. More often the bones were spread out (a skull there, a shard of rib, a cracked piece of pelvis) over a wide area, pieces always missing when I tried to reassemble them.

Another kind of skeleton I found beneath the trees were long, curved boards, bleached gray, that were the remains of old boats. People dragged them out into the woods to collapse in on themselves, to be dispersed like the bones of any other animal. And yet some were still boats, in front yards, listing to starboard in the tall golden grass along Town Line Road. The one I knew best, *Anne Maria*, sat adrift in the trees on Mr. Zahn's land, its bow just peeking out into the moonlight.

A fishing boat, its blue-and-red paint chipped and faded. Twenty feet long, with its keel stuck in the earth, so heavy that it didn't shift at all as I pulled myself up, swung a leg over onto the deck. It still smelled faintly of fish, and of diesel, though the engine was gone and so was the steering wheel in the tiny, square pilot house, behind the scratched cloudy windows all covered with registration stickers from the sixties and seventies. Most of that boat was belowdecks—a huge compartment to hold the fish, another for the nets. I lifted the cover of the latter, eased myself down, inside, and pulled the lid over the top of me.

The only sounds in that darkness were the wind in the trees and my own breathing, which helped me imagine that the boat was afloat, cruising through the trees, rising and falling along the backs of great gray swells. My arms wrapped around my knees, sitting there, I felt more than I thought, imagining the fish, still alive and drowning in the air, piled high atop each other just through the wooden partition, gasping, sliding across each other. I sailed in this landlocked boat and imagined Mr. Zahn in it, not long before, perhaps singing a song as he pulled in a net full of fish and the wind buffeted the seagulls overhead, the birds trailing the boat like a broken cloud.

The bushes outside, brushing the boat's sides, were waves, water. The slap of a leaf was the slap of a hand, just as, later that summer—as we swam among the moored boats off Ephraim, or in Nicolet Bay, or especially in the U-shaped harbor of Horse-shoe Island—Mrs. Abel would slap a boat's hull and a half-asleep owner would emerge, shouting from the deck, trying to shine lights out across the water, shouting *Who's there?* as we swam away, into the darkness.

- 8 -

At dusk, the day after I spoke with Mrs. Abel on the road, I lay on my bed in the Red Cabin and thought about her. I could hear her voice in my ears, inside my head, the teasing way she'd talked to me. I liked it, and I also liked how she'd looked, standing there on the end of the pier in the darkness—the slender, shadowy shape of her, looking out at me in the water as if waiting for me to come closer, to pull myself up next to her on the pier. Is that what she wanted? Did she want me to follow her, down the pier and across the beach and up into her cabin? And what would happen, once we were inside that space together? Would we talk? Would we climb the ladder into her loft?

Standing, ducking to keep my head from hitting the masts and sails overhead, I hurried outside, through the woods, along the shadowy paths.

I knocked on the door of Mrs. Abel's cabin. As I waited, I leaned close to peer through the window. The table, bare except for a vase holding Queen Anne's Lace, the piano, the couch, the ladder stretching up to the sleeping loft.

I tapped on the window. Still no answer.

Instead of returning to the path, home, I headed down the slope, around the cabin, toward the beach; the padlock hung loose, on the wood door to the space beneath the cabin, and I unhooked it and stepped inside, into that dark space. It smelled of dirt and old rubber; even with the door open, it took a moment for the light to seep in, for my eyes to adjust. Old fishing poles hung from the rafters, the floor joists above. Along the wall hung several black pairs of flippers, and some masks, snorkels. I picked up a mask, its rubber gasket cracked, its face cloudy; I held it up, snapped it around my head. I put a snorkel's mouthpiece between my teeth, listened to my strange, hollow breathing.

I took off the mask, the snorkel, put them away.

The stairs to the trap door were steep, almost a ladder. Slowly, I climbed them. I expected the door to be locked from above, but when I pushed up I could feel that it was not. Still, it was heavy—the weight of the floorboards, along with that of the coiled rag rug—and lifted it only a few inches, then a few more, until I could see a piece of the room. Colors—blue and green—slid along the floor, near my face; bending my neck, I could see to the window, where the sun shone through beach glass. Pieces hung from fishing line, holes drilled into them, catching the light and passing it through, clustered against the window like a strange school of fish.

It was then I heard the breathing, became aware of the sound of breathing in the room. I held still. I listened. It was her; it had to be her. The breathing was the only sound, slow and rhythmic. She was asleep, in the loft above me. Carefully, silently I let the trap door down. I retreated down the ladder, out onto the beach. I didn't look back until I was several houses away.

Later that night, once it was dark, I swam back and forth, short laps in the water in front of her cabin. The lake was calm; the moon was lost in the clouds. No one could easily see me.

I was waiting, I was swimming, breathing to one side, then the other. I didn't see Mrs. Abel come out of her house or cross the beach; she was simply there, suddenly at the end of her pier. I swam closer. I stood there, chest-deep.

"Here you are," she said.

She wore a dark robe, held a towel in her hand. She dropped the towel, undid the robe's sash and dropped the robe atop the pier. Even in the darkness I could see she wore no suit, and I turned to look away, offshore.

She pulled a swim cap over her head with a snap. She was coming backward down the ladder, the pale skin of her leg, her hip and side, closer to me, her body disappearing beneath the dark water.

"Did I startle you?" she said, laughing.

"What?"

"Isn't that one of the main reasons to swim at night?" she said.

"What?"

"Skinny-dipping," she said.

"My suit's just a Speedo," I said. "I'm fine."

"Come *on*," she said.

We were ten feet apart, only our heads above the surface, the water a black line at her neck. She was silent, as if waiting.

Finally I untied the drawstring, slipped off my suit and hung it by a leg hole from one of the posts of Mrs. Abel's pier. Behind me, I heard her kick, the sharpness of her strokes as she swam away from me. I had no choice except to start after her, to catch up.

We swam south—past our raft, past the Reeves' raft, past Harbor House, past my grandparents'. Beyond Peterson's Point, the lakebed dropped away and we fell into a rhythm, further from shore, over the deeper water.

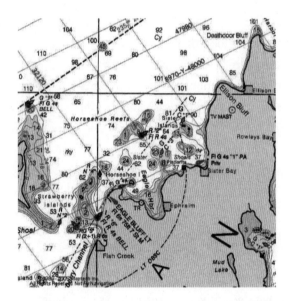

Once or twice we were close enough that I felt the kick, the water pushed away from her body, but we never touched, we never collided, the space between us elastic, the sky above dark gray, close, the trees onshore darker, the water darker still. And cold, cold at this depth. The only way to stay warm was to keep moving, and we did, out across Eagle Harbor, the village of Ephraim to our left, a mile away.

I was anxious, afraid that I'd lose her, that she'd leave me, that I'd be unable to keep up, yet after half a mile or so I relaxed, breathing every third stroke, every fourth, shifting to a breast-stroke for a moment to spot her, to see over the low waves.

We moved closer together, we drifted further apart, aware of each other, not losing track. Two dark figures swimming parallel under a darkening sky, a mile from shore.

We didn't pause until we reached Eagle Bluff, the gray cliff stretching far overhead, the one jagged hole a hundred feet overhead—that cave was visible from our shore, almost two miles away.

"Perfect night," she said.

"Yes."

We were treading water, gasping a little. Out by Horseshoe Island, lights slid along, boats easing into the harbor. In the other direction, the lights of the ice cream place, Wilson's, in Ephraim, and those of the boats in the yacht harbor. The village looked sleepy; it was past midnight, only the two of us out there.

"How old are you?" she said.

"Twenty-six."

The stars overhead, we floated on our backs, drifted into each other, touched awkwardly and drifted apart, still close enough to talk.

"When I was your age," she said, "I swam from Northport to Washington Island, by myself, one night. There are cliffs there, at the end of the peninsula. I saw cliff paintings, once. Above the waterline, on the cliff. Someone in a canoe must have painted them."

"You swam across Death's Door?"

"Over the wrecks, yes. During the day I'd dive down, through them."

It was silent, then, only the sound of the water as the waves lifted us up and dropped us down, the lake's surface breathing.

"Did you know my husband?" she said.

"I knew who he was," I said. "I never really talked to him."

"I met my husband when I was swimming. I was far from shore, and he saw me, from his boat."

I treaded water, a chill returning to my skin.

"I miss him so much," she said. "I just thought we'd have more time. But walking helps, swimming helps. Distractions are helpful."

We started back, and I was more confident than when we'd set out. It also eased my anxiety to know where we were going, and how far. I led her part of the way, out from the shadow of the cliff, glancing back once to see the thin skeleton of the tower atop the cliff—almost a hundred feet high, but so much higher above the lake. I tried to imagine if someone atop the tower might see the two of us, now, two tiny black shapes crawling slowly across that expanse. Closer together, further apart, never quite losing each other.

From Eagle Tower, which is in Peninsula State Park, a person can see for miles. The treetops, the islands, the boats, our cabin and our neighbors' cabins, our white curve of rocky shoreline. Far away. Mostly it is the miles and miles of water, torn by waves, stretched tight by currents, all shades of blue and green.

As a child I'd climb all those flights of zigzagging wooden stairs, past all those metal braces and bolts, and back then (like my daughters, now) I could not see above the top railing and had to squint between the lower ones. I can still feel that splintery wood against my face, my lips, the smell and taste of it, and the names carved into it, and dates, threats, and promises. (I never carved my name. I never sneaked up there late at night with a girlfriend, stripped down beneath the stars like my friends sometimes did. They showed me the splinters to verify their boasts.) I remember how the waving treetops below made it seem the whole thing swayed. Our car far below, the pale tan square of its rooftop in the parking lot.

As I thought of the tower, swimming away from it, I was also aware of Mrs. Abel, off to my left. We swam. In the moonlight, the long curve of her back broke the surface of the water, glowing for an instant, slipping away again. Closer to the lights we swam, closer to our houses, into the shallows.

Mrs. Abel climbed up the ladder and stood on her pier, above me. She pulled the swimming cap from her head, then wrung water from her hair. Her pale skin blended into the white stones on the beach behind her, and then she reached for her towel, her robe.

"You're not a bad swimmer," she said. "You swam in college?"

"High school," I said.

"Pool swimming's so different," she said. "The painted line on the bottom, all that back and forth."

I'd taken my suit from where it was hooked on the pier and was awkwardly trying to balance on one foot, to pull it on. Now that I was no longer swimming, I began to shiver. I couldn't tell if I should also get up on the pier, or if I should wait for her to direct me, to invite me inside, or what would happen next.

"What are you thinking about?" she said.

"Nothing," I said.

"We'll do it again," she said, and turned, walking away without looking back, disappearing into the shadows beneath the trees.

I stayed there for a moment, long enough to see candlelight flicker in the window, and then I turned and began the short swim back to our pier, our cabin.

The glassed-in porch was alight as I walked up the stone steps from the beach. I could see my father there, sitting at his desk, reading. It was likely he was reading economics, John Maynard Keynes; it was equally likely that he was reading *Hoard's Dairyman*, or fairy tales, or had fallen asleep with Blake's "Songs of Innocence and Experience" in his lap.

My father can do many things that I cannot, and falling asleep easily is one of them. When I was a boy, trying to fall asleep, he read to me. He read stories to me before I could read them for myself. He read all of *The Chronicles of Narnia* to my brother and me, and *The Lord of the Rings* and *Watership Down*. By far our favorite was Ursula Le Guin's *Earthsea Trilogy*. From it we learned that there are deep secrets, worlds behind and beyond this one, and that knowing your real name, knowing yourself, was a power to seek and a knowledge, if it can be found and held, to guard.

- 9 -

Today, I walk through the sunny streets, past a tattoo shop, a taqueria, a terrarium store, a head shop named Vapelandia. I go through a blue door and wait for my isolation tank to be readied.

An elderly, white-haired lady tells me she's waiting for her son. We sit together, on a bright yellow couch; a few minutes later, her son arrives: about my age, heavyset, with gray hair cut close to his scalp; his thick eyeglasses are almost like goggles, heavily bound—with duct and electrical tape—at the bridge and temples.

"What is this supposed to do for me, again?" the mother asks.

"What it does for me." He mumbles huskily when he speaks, seeming unable to control his volume; he is not easy to understand.

I listen in, taking off my watch, taking out my contact lenses, preparing myself. I pick up the notebook on the table, pretend to read the entries that previous, fellow travelers have left behind.

"Sleep," the son says to his mother. "It helped me. Remember when I didn't sleep for two years?"

I am led to my room, my tank. I take off my clothes, shower, slip into the tank that is lit by blue lights under the water; they cast my black, shadowy silhouette directly above me, as if I have left my body or it has left me. I stare up at it, so familiar and so foreign, suspended and exposed, and then I reach out, switch off the lights and slip into the darkness, the deep silence. The density of the water, it counteracts gravity; the temperature of the water, neither hot nor cold, blurs the edge of my body—there is no sight nor sound, no gravity or proprioception, no tactile stimulation, no speech. All these areas of my brain are inactive, gone dark, and beneath and beyond them, what is left?

What is taken away is the moment, the apprehension of the present. My brain settles somewhere between sleep and wakefulness. What remains is the past, the future, the hypothetical, and all the impressions that have been hidden beneath the surface.

I come here, I spend these hours trying to recollect, to see what will find me as I float in the black silence, a space that is not a space, where I am both naked and have no body. What I am, there and then, I don't think there's a word for it. A receptor, a traveler, a magnet. I drift back, I try to find a way forward. I listen to my breathing, I follow it, I try to clear that space and once I feel alone again, less crowded, I cannot escape my heart. The sound of it, and the reverberations it sends through my body, through that thick water. The sound of my heart doesn't stop, all around me.

What else I hear: the sound of water, and then I see the stream, slipping beneath the narrow bridge I'm crossing. A pail of blackberries swings heavy, hot in one hand. I look up and see the loose black strands of my wife's hair, wet against her pale neck. Her legs are bare, scratched by thorns and brambles, walking ahead of me. On the other side of the bridge, we come to a tree whose thick trunk is surrounded by white slices of bread, and cinnamon rolls; dog food is scattered everywhere, and plastic pails of dark grease hang from low branches. Someone is baiting a bear, luring it here to shoot it. As we stand there, considering the tree, endangered by the whole situation, rain begins to fall in scattered, heavy drops around us. It thickens, it slaps the top of my head as I run after my wife, up the gravel road, toward the house. No one sits in the two rocking chairs on the porch, but they are sawing furiously back and forth under the weight of the rain.

And then, blackness everywhere. Silence. My heartbeat becomes so relentless; I feel waves, turbulence; salt kicks up on my face. I lose any sense of the edges of my body. I am at the bottom of the lake, resting on my back on the lakebed, so deep that there is only blackness above me. I fold my body away; my legs first, then my arms and finally my torso, the whole thing like a thin blanket that fits there, just beneath the thin plate of my face. And then the music seeps up through that thick water, sounding, feeling like a huge creature is awakening, far beneath me, unfolding itself, beginning to surface.

I shower, put on my clothes, stumble out through the hallway with the colors so bright around me. I see the mother and son again, their hair wet, sitting beside each other on the yellow couch. I linger near the kombucha tap so I can overhear their conversation.

"I wear earplugs all the time, now, everywhere," he is saying. "It's all too much for me, everything coming at me all at once."

- 10 -

The second time Mrs. Abel and I swam together, we went out to and around Horseshoe Island, silently through its harbor, past the moored boats where people slept, then back toward shore, two miles in the darkness with the rolling swells pushing us along.

When we returned to her pier, she took off her bathing cap while still in the water; she held onto the ladder and leaned back; her hair eased out and settled sleekly along her head as she surfaced. Then she climbed up to the pier. She stood there above me, for a moment, before picking up her towel.

"Come inside," she said.

"I don't have any clothes," I said, pulling on my Speedo beneath the water.

"We'll find something. Come."

I followed her down the pier, across the beach, up the slope, around the side of her cabin. At the porch, she told me to wait; she returned with a towel and held the door open.

I watched as she lit the candles, the kerosene lantern, then climbed into the loft. The skin of her bare back flashed white as she dropped the towel, moved beyond where I could see.

Standing there, I was uncertain if I was supposed to, if she expected me to follow her up the ladder. I felt as I wasn't quite in my body, or in control of it. I had fantasized about this, being alone with her in her house; here I was, and instead of doing anything I was paralyzed by disbelief.

There was only the sound of waves, gently lapping at the shore. I turned away from the ladder, toward the picture of the cabin and the fire in the forest.

"Did you tear this from a book?" I said.

"Tear what?"

"This picture of the fire."

"My husband must have—it's from before we were married. Here." Suddenly she was closer, tossing clothes from the loft, then stepped back out of view again. "These should fit you, close enough."

I bent down and picked up the clothes, then stepped under the loft, kicked off my wet suit and pulled on the pants, buttoned the shirt.

In a moment, Mrs. Abel returned down the ladder. She wore a long white nightgown; when she stood close to the lamp I could see her body, a dark shadow—her slender legs, the bend of her knees; the points of her hips pushed out against the fabric, and the fabric along her shoulders was wet from her hair, translucent, her skin shining through.

"It's strange," she said, "seeing you in my husband's clothes."

I just stood there. I almost said how awkward I felt; I wasn't sure if saying it would make me more or less anxious, if it would speed or change what was going to happen.

"What's the matter?" she said.

"I didn't say anything."

"Your face," she said. "Your expression. The clothes are clean—it's not as if they're the ones he died in or something."

The kerosene lamp whispered a crinkly sigh, went silent again. I set my wet swimsuit down on the floor atop the towel. Mrs. Abel was combing out her hair; when she was done, she began to braid it. She stepped closer to me, closed the distance, and I was uncertain if I was supposed to move closer, as well. The pants she'd given me were khakis that were too short, the waist too wide so they slid down. The denim shirt was scratchy, its shoulders narrow.

And then she walked past me, sat down at the table. "You remind me of him, a little," she said. "My husband. It's not just the clothes. But you said you didn't know him?"

"Not really," I said. "If he drove past on the road, we'd wave."

"He liked to tell stories, too," she said. "Sometimes he wrote them down, sent them to me, back when I was a girl."

"I thought you hadn't known him very long," I said.

"Why did you think that?"

"That's what I heard."

"I knew him a long time," she said. "It's true that we weren't married for long, but we knew each other for years, since I was a girl."

"Okay," I said.

"Sit down," she said. "You're making me nervous."

I sat on the couch and she turned her chair, slightly, to face me.

"I was what, fourteen?" she said. "I was a teenager, I know, and swimming. I don't know why I was so far south, but I was far offshore and I could hear a boat coming, the propeller through the water. When I looked up, I could see it coming. A small, low speedboat with a pointed bow, headed right at me. And so I took a deep breath and dove deep, and held myself there, looking upward, waiting for the boat to pass over me."

I watched her, ten feet away, listened to her tell her story; her eyes faced me but they were turned inward, not watching me. She was traveling back to that time.

"I waited underwater and the boat tore the water, the surface above, and slowly began to circle. I held my breath—I stayed down there as long as I could, but at last I kicked my way up.

"He was there, standing alone in his boat. A fishing net in one hand, binoculars in the other. I was gasping, treading water, and he was reaching out with that net like he might scoop me up." Her voice rose and fell, just higher than a whisper, her face tilted as if she was in the water, looking up at the boat. "He cut the motor so I could hear what he was saying, and he was telling me to grab the net. He threw a lifejacket and I let it drift away.

"At last, at last he understood that I was swimming, that I didn't need saving. He relaxed and let his boat drift alongside as I floated on my back, and we talked."

She paused. In came the wind, the waves.

"I wouldn't tell him my name," she said. "He was shirtless, with a farmer's tan. He made a joke about mermaids, and I kicked my legs to show I didn't have a tail."

I wondered if Mrs. Abel had been wearing a bathing suit, that day. I tried to imagine Mr. Abel as a younger, middle-aged man; I could only recall him as older, talking to my grandfather as they walked along the road, both wearing cardigans, tweed driving caps on their heads. I remembered him laughing with Mr. Zahn, once, at a party, cocktails in their hands.

Now Mrs. Abel leaned forward, the sharp tips of her braids dripping water on the floorboards. "I remember that he used the word 'beguiled,'" she said. "He said that mermaids couldn't be caught, only beguiled. They had to come to a person of their own accord. He wore sunglasses, a wide hat. He pointed to the shore, pointed out his cabin, so I'd know where he lived."

"This cabin?" I said.

She looked at me, startled, as if she'd forgotten I was there. "I liked that he left me there," she said, "that he didn't try to make me come with him, take me to shore, that he didn't ask my name again." She smiled. "He put on a jacket, standing there in his boat, watching me, and the jacket was inside out so he took it off and fixed that and put it on again. Then he started the engine and sped away."

"And then what?" I said.

"After that?" She waved one hand in the air, her voice tapering off, speeding up, growing quieter. "He found out my name, somehow, and he wrote me letters, and then, much later, we were married, and then he died."

It was silent for a moment, only the gentle lapping of waves. Out the window, the moon glowed on the lake. Turning back toward Mrs. Abel, I saw a shape hanging in the air behind her, over her shoulder. Suspended from a wire, swinging from the underside of the loft. I stood, stepped closer. It was a roughly painted little airplane, carved from driftwood, with two propellers made of empty wooden thread spools. Atop the airplane's wing stood a wooden bird, painted blue and standing on legs of rusty nails.

"A friend gave it to me," she said. "He carved it."

"Oh," I said, uncertain what to say next. I kept staring at the bluebird as I felt her watching me, waiting for something. It was as if the wind had suddenly dropped away, as if the waves had all suddenly fallen calm.

"What are you doing here?" she said.

"What do you mean?"

"You seem so nervous."

"I'm not," I said.

"I heard a funny story about you," she said, after a long moment. "About a summer a couple years ago. I heard you came back from college with beautiful long hair, and all the women on the shore envied it, and you got so much attention, but your girlfriend—a girl from Little Sister Bay—made you cut it off."

"She didn't make me," I said. "She, that was a while ago. A long time."

I was still standing there, underneath the loft; I reached out and touched the wooden bird and the airplane swung back and forth, the raspy sound of the wire in its hook.

"So you've had other girlfriends, since then?" She said the word *girlfriends* as if the term was one she found funny.

"Yes," I said.

"A lot?"

"I don't know."

"You've forgotten?"

"A normal amount."

"What's normal?"

"Just a regular number."

"Sounds passionate!" She laughed at me again. "*Serious* girl-friends?"

"Now it doesn't seem like it."

"But then it did."

"I guess so. Yes."

"But not now?"

"No," I said. "Not for a while."

Mrs. Abel stood and walked around the table. She looked out the window, over the lake.

"That girl," I said. "I talked to her last year and she told me she still had my hair, the ponytail that was cut off, that she kept it in a jewelry box."

"How romantic," Mrs. Abel said. "Unless she's planning on putting a hex on you."

"I was still in college when all that happened," I said.

"And now you're grown up?"

"No," I said.

Around us, candle flames flickered in the draft. The kerosene lantern glowed atop the piano.

"But you're twenty-six," Mrs. Abel said. "You're out of college."

"So what have I been doing?" I said, anticipating the question. "I moved to Montana to work on a ranch, and then I moved to New York because I had a girlfriend who went to graduate school."

"But not the same girlfriend who kept your hair?"

"No," I said.

"And where is she now, this graduate school girlfriend?"

"Canada," I said.

"Canada," Mrs. Abel said. "You think she'll return?"

"I don't know," I said. "I don't think that's really going on anymore."

I could see the shape of myself, standing there awkwardly, in the reflection of the window. Mrs. Abel leaned close to the glass, then, her hand up to block the glare, so she could look out at the lake.

"It's late," she said, turning toward me.

There was only the faint sound of waves, wind in the trees.

"Okay." I nodded at her, moved toward the door. "I'll bring back these clothes."

"It doesn't matter," she said. "I don't know why I've kept them—they don't even smell like him, anymore."

I stepped out, onto the porch, and closed the door behind me. Before I had crossed her driveway and entered the shadows beneath the trees, though, I heard the door open again.

I turned; she stood there in the moonlight, reaching out for me, but as I came closer I realized there was something in her hands—my swimsuit, still damp.

"You wouldn't want to forget this," she said.

"Thanks."

"Goodnight." She turned, closed the door behind her.

Walking away from her cabin, into the woods, I paused, half-expecting her to be watching me, or to call me back again. The glow in the windows diminished gradually, as she blew out the candles, one by one; and then the windows disappeared, the cabin a dark silhouette against the night. For a moment I wondered if I should go back, if she had actually wanted me to leave (*I guess you should go*, she'd said).

What did she want me for? To push back her sadness, to be another distraction, like walking the highway at night, swimming through the dark water? I could do that, I thought; I could be that. Still, I didn't quite have the nerve to turn, to return to her cabin that night.

- 11 -

Notes toward stories, from the summer of 1994:

—I wanted to part the ground and swim just beneath the surface.

—Treating physical objects that caused injury as injury itself (e.g. bandaging knife).

—Riding my bicycle, I rode over a snake and its head jerked up to strike as my tire rolled over its body, but it missed and I pedaled away, hard. When I circled back, I saw that the snake was long dead, dried and flattened, not alive at all.

—Stories where initial crises lead to long digressions that never really return to the opening but the motion subtly bears on possible implications of opening.

—Her skin felt smooth and tight around her bones, crisp, her temples rang. Surfacing, she whooped and it echoed along the cliff, traveling up and down the beach. She brought her hands in close to her body, back through the straps of her bathing suit, and peeled it down, slipping it off as she swam, letting it slide down her legs and leaving it to float behind like a strange jellyfish.

—A person who sits in their house and practices different expressions; coupled with someone who lives nearby and watches, drawing conclusions.

- 12 -

A year or so ago, one August afternoon, I walked through those woods with my daughters, visiting the forts and hide-outs from the stories I'd told them. The girls followed me to the Red Cabin, seeking to find a canoe paddle or bicycle—it's mostly used for storage, now. And while we still call it the Red Cabin, several years ago it was painted a flat, dark gray.

The screen door opened with the exact same sound, that terrible shriek. By the door, a bike—my Schwinn Cruiser, from college—hung upside down. It's still there, its whitewall tires off its rims, its seat half eaten away. And the sails are still there, unused for years, far away from the wind of the lake. And the Montana license plates from my long ago truck.

Tacked to the wall above the desk, yellowed slips of paper:

A passage from the journals of Albert Camus ("It is only in order to shine sooner that the author refuses to rewrite. Despicable. Begin again.");

A rejection letter from C. Michael Curtis at *The Atlantic* ("July 6, 1994: Still no luck, but thanks for the look.");

A passive-aggressive quotation out of a letter from Hemingway to Fitzgerald ("Summer's a discouraging time to work—You don't feel death coming on the way it does in the fall when the boys really put pen to paper.");

A postcard photograph of a weathered Cormac McCarthy, sent from a friend whose first book was being published, who had his picture taken by the same photographer as Cormac. She'd given him the postcard. *Glad to hear you happy, friend. It eludes me, it does, but we still have time don't we?*

My daughters—bored with all this musty detritus, the spider webs everywhere—spilled back outside, began playing on the dangerous balance beams my father had set up, so long ago, and climbing on the small stone table we'd built, once, in honor of Aslan and Narnia.

Standing in the Red Cabin, surrounded by the artifacts of that other person, by my old things, I felt a sense of dislocation, caught between times, in two times at once.

My daughters laughed and shouted, impatient beneath the cedars. Before I opened the screen door, I leaned close to the wall, to look into another faded piece of paper tacked there:

It's a photocopy of a photograph of a handless, blind boy reading Braille with his lips—I always had this with me; there are rusted holes along its top border, from the various tacks and nails that affixed it to the walls above the tables and desks where I wrote, as I moved from place to place in those years. I wanted my writing to be worthy of such a boy, a reader who would kiss every letter of every word.

Was I oblivious to the pretension of this gesture, blind myself to the insensitivity it displayed? I fear I was. I suspect that perhaps this picture was as much for other people to see—to be disturbed and impressed—as it was to inspire me.

- 13 -

One night in that first week of swimming with Mrs. Abel, I was walking through the woods. In the darkness I felt a familiarity, an awareness of all my childhood forts and hideouts (Chipmunk, Bat, Porcupine) around me, a sense that I was in tune with the mysteries. Again I crossed the road and headed up the old cow path, slanting along the bluff. Again, near the top of the path, light spilled out of Mr. Zahn's screen porch. I slowed as I passed. The old man was still out there, and as I began to shout hello I realized that he was in the exact same position as he had been, several nights before. Sitting there, slightly slumped, that knife in one hand. He had not moved at all.

I stepped closer, I reached out and scratched my fingernail against the bristly screen, hoping to rouse him.

"Mr. Zahn?"

There were stone steps, a screen door around the side of the porch. I let myself in. I did not get very close to him; I did not touch him, and yet I was close enough to see his pale scalp through his white hair, the strands of gray tangled in his long white beard. His blue eyes were open, milky, but they weren't seeing anything. He wasn't breathing, didn't seem to be. His body was perfectly still.

The house creaked, startling me. I glanced through a doorway, into a dark room. It was silent again.

Wood shavings covered the floor around Mr. Zahn's heavy boots. A half-carved bird was clutched in the hand that didn't hold the knife. His plaid shirt, his suspenders, liver spots along the edge of his face. A breeze shifted through the screens and then I could smell him.

Turning away, I stared through the doorway, into the dark room, silhouettes I couldn't decipher.

When I turned on the light, the creatures leapt up—birds and deer and skunks and raccoons. All carved in wood, roughly painted. A carved deer with real antlers, with wooden birds along its back. Birds. Woodpeckers, bald eagles, sparrows, orioles. Deer with blue eyes, human-like, made of cloudy beach glass. Weathered sea captains, woodsmen with red caps, people with nails pounded into their wooden heads, to look like hair.

I didn't step into that room; my hand was still on the light switch; I kept Mr. Zahn in my peripheral vision, sitting where he was sitting, that knife in his hand. Near my feet, a carved badger with what appeared to be dentures for teeth, bottle caps for eyes. Snakes, coiled and straight, but mostly it was birds—legs of wire, beaks of glass, wings bent from tin cans that reflected the light until I switched the switch.

I left Mr. Zahn with his light on, sitting there in the porch like I'd found him. Carefully I opened the screen door, stepped outside again. By the time I reached the cow path I was already running.

I don't know how much time passed, or even if I went there directly, but I found myself standing in Mrs. Abel's rutted driveway. Candlelight flickered in the windows and the sound of the piano—a simple, repetitive melody—faintly slipped out around the cabin, under the trees where I was standing. I think I called out, but I didn't want to raise my voice, really, to draw anyone else's attention. So I moved closer, to where I could see her inside, sitting alone at the piano.

Her face was lit, flickering, and her hair was in two thick braids, one hanging down her back, the other in front of her shoulder, its tip almost brushing the piano keys.

When I knocked, the music stopped, and after a moment the door jerked open.

"Oh, it's you," she said. "Did you want to swim?"

"It's not me," I said. "I mean, not swimming. It's Mr. Zahn. Something's happened."

Mrs. Abel's face was so calm, looking into mine. Gray strands showed among the black in her braids.

"He's—" I said. "I think he's dead."

"Show me," she said.

We didn't speak; I don't remember if we spoke as we hurried through the dark forest, along the road, up the path. I do remember what Mrs. Abel said, as soon as we were in that screen porch where Mr. Zahn had been waiting.

"Oh, Robert," she said.

"You know him?" I said.

"Yes," she said. "I did."

A fly buzzed around the ceiling, the screens, and I watched it, afraid that it would land on Mr. Zahn, settle on his face, crawl into his ear or nose. The buzzing was so loud and I stood there, uncertain how to stop it. Finally the fly landed on the screen door, and I stepped quickly to open it. The sound was gone.

"Are you leaving?" Mrs. Abel said, turning toward the door.

"No," I said. "It was the fly."

"What?"

"Nothing," I said.

"What should we do?" When she said this it seemed like she was asking herself, or Mr. Zahn, not really expecting an answer from me. "He does have children," she said, after a moment. "None that live too close."

She glanced over at Mr. Zahn as if he might disagree. And then at the same time as it seemed he might interrupt us, startle himself back to life and resume his carving, it also began to feel familiar, a situation that was not unexpected.

Mrs. Abel stood; she reached out and for a moment it seemed she was going to touch him, but instead she touched the carved headrest of his chair. She ran her hand along the top of a small table, its drawers and feet carved to look like lions' heads.

"I think he's been here, like this," I said. "I didn't know. I saw him the other night, but I thought he was sleeping. I didn't know."

She had stepped closer to me, and I thought I felt her touch my bare arm, but then it seemed she was not that close, too far away to reach me.

"It's more sad," I said. "It's sadder, that he was sitting here, these days—"

"It's all the same," she said. "It doesn't matter to him." After a moment, she said, "You should go."

"I can stay."

Mrs. Abel crossed the room, slid the knife from the old man's gnarled fingers, then folded the blade away and put it in her pocket. She looked up at me.

"Go home," she said, her voice a whisper. "I'll take care of this."

I glanced back once, from the cow path. Mr. Zahn still sat there in his plaid shirt and suspenders, his tangled white beard and hair. Mrs. Abel pulled a chair up and sat next to him, the two of them facing out, motionless, staring through the screen and into the dark trees of the night.

TWO

- 14 -

The painter Charles Burchfield once buried a dead bird with a note that read *Music exists in other forms*. In his journal, he writes, "I saw a reflection of a falling cherry petal in a window and thought how like it was [to] the bird's life." He imagines that a "fairy, building a house of the wings of a moth, might use the transparent spots in the wings as windows. What would flowers look like seen thru them!"

My daughters are always looking for fairies, scouring our neighborhood, searching for signs, evidence of these creatures' existence.

The other day, a dead hummingbird appeared, resting on its back, on a small table just outside our window. I saw the girls pick it up and carry it around; they were talking to it, but I couldn't hear what they were saying.

I stood inside the house, close against the curtains where they couldn't see me, and watched them. They leaned their faces close to the bird, whispering. They set it gently down.

Friends of mine once belonged to a church in Montana whose beliefs described how we come from beyond, and live many lives. One of their practices was to listen carefully to a child's first words, and to hesitate in correcting them. Our tendency is to try to bring a child's understanding into alignment with this imperfect world, when their understanding, incomprehensible to us, is coming from a truer place, or may speak from the experiences of a previous life.

I watched my girls with pride and tenderness, it's true, but also with envy. I knew that if I slid the glass door open, their whispering would stop; they would look up at me with innocent exasperation and quickly cease whatever they were doing.

Later, I found the grave where they'd buried the hummingbird, back against the fence, next to the rhododendron. A plank of wood leaned there, a heart drawn on it with black marker.

- 15 -

The day after I left Mrs. Abel with Mr. Zahn on that screen porch, I went to her house. I felt what had happened, that shared experience, had changed things between us, somehow, perhaps deepened them.

But she was not there.

That night, I swam back and forth in the dark water off her pier. No candlelight flickered in the windows of her cabin.

On the second day it was the same, and on the third, at dusk, I followed the paths through the woods again; I didn't knock on her door—instead, I went along the side of the house, down the slope that led to the lake. I unhooked the open padlock from the wooden doors and stepped into the darkness. Shadows eased to reveal the black triangles of the flippers that hung on the wall. The dull glint of the masks' round faces, the dark crooks of snorkels.

Closing the door behind me, I fumbled for the rungs of the ladder, then began to climb. The trap door was unlocked, and I eased it open, its weight heavy in my palms, along the top of my head. If she were sleeping, I decided, I'd go inside; quietly, so as not to wake her, and then I would wait until she did awaken, and I would be there, and we would talk.

I lifted the trapdoor only a few inches, just enough so I could see through the gap, my eyes at the level of the floor. I hesitated, expecting to see her moccasins step into view, standing there, the rest of her hidden, above, awaiting some explanation. I listened. There was nothing, no movement, not even the sound of breathing.

One end of the spiral rag rug lay heavily atop the door; when I lifted, it slid away, and then a chair tipped over, bouncing on the floor with several loud cracks. I waited, the trap door still balanced atop my head, and let the silence settle. Then I slipped in, slithering on my belly and standing up quickly, turning a slow circle to be certain I was alone.

The room felt crowded, and there was a chemical scent in the air. I rested one hand on the cool rung of the ladder to the loft, its wood worn smooth by her fingers. My eyes adjusted to the light. There—in the corner next to the piano stood a side table; closer, I recognized it as the table from Mr. Zahn's screen porch, the lions' heads carved on the drawer pulls. I ran my hand along the dark, smooth wood.

Gray light eased through the windows; voices still called from the lake, and the sound of motorboats, the last waterskiing before dark.

On the piano I noticed a blue can of WD-40, which accounted for the smell, and walked into the kitchen, opening cupboards— her few mismatched glasses and canning jars, chipped plates—and jerking open drawers, the sound of clattering silverware filling that small space. On the counter stood a pitcher of water, two apples in a bowl; taking one, I bit into it as I turned and walked back into the other room.

And then I knew that I'd been mistaken, that she was in the loft, sleeping silently or merely being quiet, seeing what I would do.

"Hello?" I said.

Slowly, I climbed that short ladder, peered up into the loft. It was empty, only enough room for the mattress. I reached out and touched the worn blue blanket, pinching the fabric between my fingers. Stepping up a rung, I sank my face into the one pillow. Its case was pale yellow, and it smelled of bleach, not of Mrs. Abel. Did Mrs. Abel actually have a scent? Would I recognize it?

I heard a sound—footsteps, out on the gravel driveway.

Quickly, I climbed down.

When the door opened, when she stepped into the room, I was standing awkwardly next to the table with that half-eaten apple in my hand, not sure what to say.

Mrs. Abel only nodded, as if she expected to find me there. She looked tired, older than I thought of her looking. One of her braids had come half undone.

"I'm sorry," I said.

We stood there for a moment, silence settling between us.

"I've been talking to his family," she said, and her voice was so soft that I thought she might cry, but she did not. "Some of his children, explaining what happened."

I expected her to light candles, the kerosene lantern, but she did not. She sat down at the piano and played a scale, high on the keyboard. The silence shifted, then settled again. Out the window the sky was turning darker.

"His table," I said, to say something. "How did you get it down here?" I reached out and pulled on one of the wooden lions' heads, but the drawer didn't open. It was locked somehow.

"Here." Mrs. Abel stood from the piano bench, brushed past me. "See."

She demonstrated how the drawers worked; they stayed locked unless you gripped the sides of the lions' jaws, and then they slid open easily, smoothly. One drawer was empty, and the other held the pocketknife I'd seen her take from his hand. Silver at the ends, with a brown-and-white bone handle. I picked it up, heavier than I expected, and opened the sharp, shiny blade.

Without a word, Mrs. Abel took it back from me, folded away the blade. She set the knife in the drawer again and slid the drawer closed.

Other lions were carved down lower, on the table's braces. Bending to one knee, I grasped their jaws and slid open the two small, secret compartments. Both empty.

"I'm so tired." Mrs. Abel stepped away and stood there, next to the ladder that stretched up to the loft. "Too tired to swim, if that's what you wanted. I need to sleep."

- 16 -

The creatures come to life. The wooden birds with their jerky wings, the deer with its blue beach-glass eyes, its stiff legs kicking the walls as it rattles around the room. Inside Mr. Zahn's house, and I am in it, too, caught in the center of the room while I am asleep. It is as if the animals can't escape; shining wings, serrated, cut from the lids of cans, scratch the walls, the ceiling. Wood splinters, cracks. When they brush against me, I feel feathers, not metal. I feel fur, not painted wood. A badger with human dentures for teeth scurries over my feet, a tiny sea captain with nails for hair totters past. Fishing boats the size of boots sail across the floor, up the walls, along the ceiling. The birds rise in a flock, spinning and collapsing tightly together, wheeling, and I stumble through to open the door to let them loose.

And I open my eyes, expecting the dark shapes of bicycles above me, hanging upside down in the Red Cabin, the shadowy windsurfer sails, twisted around their masts. Instead, there's the sound of my wife breathing beside me in the darkness, the curve of her bare shoulder, her familiar shape beneath the blankets. Down the hallway, the rustling of the guinea pigs in their cage.

I try not to awaken my wife as I cross the bedroom, open the door, head toward the kitchen. Once the coffee is started, I check my email; there's a message from an old girlfriend I've not heard from in some time. She writes:

> Yesterday I was in a sensory deprivation tank and experienced six very vivid brief hallucinations, each like a still photograph. One of them was of the small strip-mart where we did our laundry and ate brunch, in Ithaca, I think. Was it really called Suds Your Duds? I could see the edge of the truck and your hand on the steering wheel and little golden hairs sticking up on your wrist, and then part of the sign. It was a very strange brain event. I still have every letter you wrote for when you donate your literary papers to the Beinecke. Love to you and yours & hope to see you sometime soon.

When I admit that I no longer have the letters she sent to me, she writes:

> I wish you'd burned my letters in a fit of rage! I wish you were angrier at me, because it would make sense of things a little more, but maybe you were then, and you would have mellowed now anyways. I have a very difficult time understanding what and how I thought of the future during that time. I sincerely have about as

much access to my state of mind during those years after college as I do to my cat's.

The end of that relationship—that was just before the same summer I've been trying to recollect. For some reason, in trying to recall what happened with Mrs. Abel, I've hardly thought about or I've tried to avoid the fact that I was slipping away from, had been slipping away from, a relationship that had lasted for years, from college in Connecticut to Montana to upstate New York. I've not even considered the momentum that carried me into that summer. I wrote to her:

I've actually been thinking about that time, that summer after we parted, looking through artifacts, trying to figure out what was up with me or who I was, then.

Trying to write about what happened with us?

Not exactly.

Should I send you the letters?

The ones I wrote, you mean?

I'd want them back, if I sent them to you.

The letters were in a box in her house in Toronto, and she now lives in Los Angeles, where she's a successful screenwriter, television writer. Her renter in Canada could not easily find the letters;

in the delay, my feelings about reading them began to change. I began to wonder if my attempt to understand the past was merely encouraging and allowing bad behavior in the present. I lost sleep over this; in the end, I thanked her for keeping the letters, and asked her not to send them to me.

She wrote back:

After you left did you ever think we might reconcile? Is it true that the words "breaking up" were never spoken between us?

Reconcile is such a strange word. I don't know that we really broke up (not that we're still together!). I wasn't really thinking of us as at a moment where we had been a couple and then we weren't a couple. I just kind of felt we were moving in different directions—literally. Is that too vague and slippery? I really didn't know, even then, about a future that was far away; all I knew is that we were going to be apart with no plans to get back together. It was months later, when I was in Wisconsin, and I distinctly remember walking around outside the cabin with a cordless phone, and you were in Canada saying (I feel bad about this) "Everything else in my life is clear and it's good, except this thing with us. Did we break up? Are we breaking up?" and I was like "I guess so, I mean, I don't know when we'll be in the same place." I was moving so intuitively and wasn't right for a while, to be certain. Maybe it would've been much healthier if I understood how to break up? For me to know what I wanted, though, might be too much to ask at that time.

Was it that you met someone else, that summer?

No. It wasn't anything like that.

- 17 -

The passages I copied down from books that summer—I still have the notebooks—largely revolve around and concern themselves with love and longing. I can see the jagged excitement of my handwriting where I transcribed these lines from Rilke:

> *For one to love another human being: that is perhaps the most difficult task that has been given to us, the ultimate, the final product and proof, the work for which all other work is merely preparation . . . Love does not at first mean merging, surrendering, and uniting with another person . . . Rather, it is high inducement for the individual to ripen, to become something in himself, to become world, to become world in himself for another's sake.*

Those words resonated as some kind of promise inside me as I churned through that black water, as I stalked through the dark woods with the wind roaring in the night branches, far overhead, as I climbed the trees and rode out the storms that came across the water, as I stood on the edge of the bluff and looked over the thick treetops shifting and swirling in the wind like another, greener lake.

(*Was I "becoming world" in those days? What would that even mean?*)

- 18 -

We swam into the black water, through it, over the depths. When I breathed to my right, I caught a glimpse of Mrs. Abel's bent arm, the stars, the distant islands and horizon. I breathed to the left and saw the lighted windows of the cabins along the shore.

Inside those cabins were our neighbors, and they were talking, in those weeks after Mr. Zahn's death, about the news that Mrs. Abel had purchased his house, along with everything in it. This, of course, sped chatter all up and down the shoreline.

Our strokes slow and steady, we swam, parallel to each other. A mile from shore, the lake remained calm, though still undulating, rising and falling in long, wide, breaker-less swells; beneath us, the lakebed might be thirty or forty or a hundred feet below, rising and falling, and the black currents twisted, fish shuttling away as we crawled across the surface. Though I knew that Mr. Zahn was already buried, up in the Moravian cemetery, as I swam I imagined his body somewhere below me, spinning in the currents, a knife glinting in one hand, his white beard floating smoothly around his face. (As if he'd been buried at sea; again, from my notebooks of that summer—a passage copied from Chekhov's "Gusev": "He went rapidly towards the bottom. Did he reach it? It was said to be three miles to the bottom. After sinking sixty or seventy feet, he began moving more and more slowly, swaying rhythmically, as though he were hesitating and, carried along by the current, moved more rapidly sideways than downward.")

I stopped once, treading water, and looked back. The lights in the houses were tiny, faint, the bluff hard to distinguish from the water, the beach impossible to see.

"What's the matter?" she said, closer than I'd expected.

"Nothing," I said.

When she turned, her foot gently kicked, brushed my ribs, and then we were heading out further, deeper. On the horizon I could see the lights of distant boats, most likely freighters heading toward the Upper Peninsula of Michigan. We found our rhythm again, the slight chill of the water receding with the effort. The blackness below, the darkness above, the way they blended together and time stretched. I could not keep count of my strokes.

And then Mrs. Abel was no longer there, to my right, and I stopped, and spun, trying to find her. The stars, the horizon, lights that could be boats or more stars. As I tried to calm myself, I finally heard her calling my name, from somewhere behind me. I swam in that direction, and then I saw her silhouette dark against the horizon. It was as if she were standing on the lake's surface.

She wasn't treading water; she was standing, stretching her arms across her chest to loosen her shoulders. She dropped her arms, put her hands on her hips. As I drew closer, I could see that the water around her was darker, moving in riffles.

"What's happening?" I said.

"A shoal," she said, the water reaching almost to her knees.

Carefully I stretched my feet into the darkness beneath me. At first, nothing, then a smooth, slanted piece of stone.

"I never knew," she said, "but I'm not exactly sure where we are, either."

Beyond her, I could barely make out faint, scattered lights on the shoreline. Was it our shoreline? It was impossible to tell the lights apart from the stars.

"How big is this?" she said.

We shuffled along the shoal, from one stone to the next. After a few minutes, I slipped off the edge, into deeper water, and I turned back, keeping Mrs. Abel in sight, moving closer to her again. My feet were scratched, half-numb; I shivered. I kept crossing the shoal, finding its edges. It was long and thin, perhaps sixty feet long and ten feet across.

Behind me, I heard Mrs. Abel begin to say something, but when I turned I could not see her. I held still, turned slowly, called her name.

I called her name again and again, and she did not answer.

Slowly, I moved along the shoal, down its length, and could not find her. I squinted into the darkness in every direction and I felt the pressure of the darkness pushing back, closing down around me so that it became difficult to breathe, to call, to shout.

How much time passed?

I shivered, I shouted, I searched, I called.

The edge of the horizon began to lighten, to glow. My teeth chattered. My hands, my feet were numb; I couldn't feel the stones beneath me, yet still I was standing. The cold of the water had returned, intensified, sharp against the edges of my skin and sinking deeper into my body.

I stepped off the edge, plunged down, surfaced gasping. And then when I turned back to the shoal, to put my feet down again, I could not find it.

I splashed, I circled. I stretched my feet into nothing, I dove deep, I floated on my back to rest, still shivering as the water tightened colder and colder, thick around me.

I had lost the shoal; I had lost her, or she had lost me.

Guessing at the direction, I finally set out alone, trying to kick blood into my feet, slapping my hands. I couldn't feel my fingers, couldn't hold them together. I swam, raking at the water, in the direction of and losing sight of lights on shore. For a time I swam on my back, trying to navigate by the stars above, to stay in alignment with them though I knew they were also moving with the rotation of the earth.

I didn't recognize the shoreline as I approached it, didn't know where I was until I was ashore. It was dawn, almost dawn. I crawled onto the beach, spread out flat on the stones with my feet still in the water. At first I didn't recognize the sound all around me was my own sobbing.

I lifted my head, looked around myself. I was halfway between Little Sister Bay and the end of our road, a stretch where the bluff was close to the lake; there was no through road, but there were a few houses, lights switching on against the morning.

I crawled up under the trees, unable to feel my hands, my feet, my face numb so that if there were tears on it I couldn't feel them.

I was stumbling naked through the woods. A dog barked. Darkness was receding, all around me. I veered in another direction. At a clothesline I stole a towel, cool and soft and smelling of detergent, and wrapped it around myself as I ran. The towel was bright red; I threw it down. Another house, its windows dark, another clothesline. A green sweatshirt, a pair of plaid shorts. My feet were thawing, beginning to hurt, all scratched up and bleeding.

Someone shouted behind me, but the voice faded. There were no more dogs barking.

I came to the path at the end of our road, and so I arrived at Mrs. Abel's cabin.

Inside, I said her name, I ran into the kitchen, back to climb the ladder to the loft, to look into that empty space.

She wasn't there. She hadn't returned.

Should I have called someone? Was I thinking that I should have called someone? I don't know. She had no phone.

I was thirsty, weak. I drank glass after glass of water, ate most of a box of saltine crackers, half a jar of peanut butter; that was all the food I could find.

Climbing halfway to the loft, I reached up and pulled a blanket loose. I twisted it around myself. I stretched out on the couch and waited for her return.

My muscles twitched, my legs kicking and arms jerking slightly beneath the blanket. My feet and hands, my fingers

ached. All across the floor of her cabin were my bloody footprints—running back and forth, searching.

When I awakened, I was swimming. I thrashed against the
blanket, kicked myself free. I'd fallen off the couch, and bright
light reflected through the window, off the lake. I stood,
stretched, checked the loft once more.

Carefully I made my way along the path through the woods,
back to the Red Cabin. There I took off my stolen sweatshirt and
shorts and changed into a T-shirt and trunks, a pair of sandals.
Then I headed down toward the lake.

My mother waved from the kitchen window, where she was
washing dishes at the sink; she shouted something, some form
of question. I just waved back, pointed toward the beach, and
kept moving.

The towel and clothes I'd left behind the night before, before
I'd swum down the shore to meet Mrs. Abel, were still on our
pier. I gathered them up, threw them into our aluminum canoe,
and then dragged the canoe down along the stones, into the lake.

I paddled out of the shallows, past the raft, out into the deeper
water where I could no longer see the bottom; straight out from
shore, not really thinking, squinting against the brightness. The
water was calm, the surface of the lake barely rippled; it was a
still day, and hot. Ahead of me, the water shimmered; light rose
and spun and dissipated.

If she were out here, I knew, I had almost no hope of finding
her. I simply didn't know what else to do except to paddle, to
listen to the lap of the water against the canoe's metal sides. My

arms and legs, my face was hot with sunburn, my muscles sore from the night before, my throat parched.

At last I turned around, back toward the familiar shoreline that hung suspended over the horizon, thick and dark; closer in, the white face of the bluff showed itself, and then the trees separated, their trunks and the shadows beneath them. At last even those shadows thinned, as I came in closer, so I could see up under the trees, the bright shapes of children playing in the woods.

Mrs. Abel's cabin looked empty—I'd been asleep, there, only hours before—and the windows glinted, reflecting back at me. Her white towel lay on the pier, left behind. I retrieved my Speedo, hooked through one leg to a post, and dropped it in the bottom of the canoe with my other things; I waited for a moment, in case she'd come out of her house or call out to me. Then I checked behind myself, shivering, as if she might suddenly surface and ask me why I'd left her.

That afternoon, I patrolled up and down the shoreline in the canoe, staring through the clear water. I saw smallmouth bass; perch with their striped sides; a school of thick carp. I saw white stones, stones skipped or thrown from the beach that would eventually be as green as those around them. I saw a lost anchor, shaped like a mushroom, rusting and trailing a shred of line.

People, neighbors waved to me from their piers, swimmers called from the raft. Probably they thought I was fishing; one pole had been left in the canoe, its white tip slanting upward. An old Zebco 202 combo, with a silver-and-blue Lil Cleo on the end of its line, that spoon swinging back and forth above the water, reflecting in it. I didn't lower it into the water, didn't cast or troll, half afraid of what I might snag.

- 19 -

Two days passed, and the following night was my father's birthday party, after which I believe we went to see *City Slickers II* and *Speed* at the Skylight Drive-In. I have no recollection of those movies—I was thinking of Mrs. Abel, worried, wondering what had happened, what I could have done, what I might say, why I wasn't saying anything. (Was it that I was afraid of being found out? If so, what would even be found out? Was it that it was a secret? How would I explain what we'd been doing, or describe our relationship, when I didn't really understand it myself? We had swum together, I could say. At night.) I also began to realize that anything I would say would be too late to help. Whatever had happened to Mrs. Abel could not be undone. I also realized that no one had missed her. Other than me, no one was used to seeing her with any regularity. Her disappearance simply wasn't noticed.

I stayed away from the lake, those days. I didn't swim at all. A few times, I checked her empty house. Mostly, though, I tried to forget what had happened, to distract myself; I tried to turn that summer into past summers, to return to my old activities, my old friends.

This wasn't easy, because by that point most of my childhood summer friends had actual jobs—in Milwaukee or Chicago or even farther away—and came up the peninsula on rare weekends, if at all. I was left to consort with the younger siblings of my friends, the little brothers and sisters. At first they were excited, honored to go out with me, but after a few nights they all knew and felt, as I did, that the arrangement was slightly pathetic. Still, it helped me to forget, for moments, as I traveled back and forth to the AC Tap, out on Highway 57, drinking Pabst and eating pickled eggs, turkey gizzards. We tossed the beanbags, played "There's a Tear in My Beer" on the jukebox, all the things I'd done a thousand times before.

One of these nights, after last call at the Tap, I passed on an opportunity to skinny-dip with the others, down off the dock in Ephraim. I let them drop me at the top of our road, so the sound of tires on our gravel driveway wouldn't awaken my parents.

I walked slowly through the moonlit shadows to the Red Cabin, where I opened the door slowly, to quiet the spring, and switched on the light. The first thing I saw, twisted in the corner, on the floor, were the clothes I'd stolen from the clotheslines. They'd been there for days, yet suddenly they struck me like an accusation, a kind of link or evidence that should not be discovered. I picked up the green sweatshirt, the khaki shorts, then found the shirt and pants—Mr. Abel's, that she'd given me—and went back out into the night, under the dark trees.

I considered burying all the clothes, but I had no shovel; I began to climb a tree, but that also seemed a poor solution. Should I pile stones on top of them? Burn them? I kept walking, past the graves of our dogs Toto Tulip and Daisy Grace, then onto the road and up the slanted path along the cliff, past Mr. Zahn's empty house.

When I reached the boat beneath the trees, I climbed up, crawled deep inside the hold where once the nets had been folded and stored. The bent wood inside the hull was smooth and cool, familiar as the faint smell of diesel, the fishiness emanating from the hull, the dampness of the lake in the past and the forest all around. I pulled the rickety hatch over the opening, closing out the stars; I curled up with the clothes beneath my head and rested there half-asleep, hardly thinking.

Eventually I was startled by branches scratching the boat's side, by the wind high above. A storm was rising. I climbed out of the hold, over the edge, leaving the clothing behind, and as I stumbled down the path the sound of waves echoed around me, all along the cliff.

At the Red Cabin, when I touched the door, a round strip of paper fell from the doorknob. It was actually a piece of birch bark (one that I still have—flattened, taped into a notebook). Inside, I switched on the light and read what had been scratched there:

where Are you?
where were you?
Are you Alright

That night the wind was blowing so hard that sticks rained down from the trees and fell around me as I made my way along the path. I could see the candlelight flickering in the windows of Mrs. Abel's cabin, but it wasn't until I was close that I heard the piano, struggling to be heard in its conversation with the storm. Rising, swelling, receding again; the melody disappeared and then returned, coming like the black line of a gust traveling across the surface of the water.

I opened the door, stepped into the room, the music so much louder, inside. She didn't hear, didn't notice me as I stood behind her. Her hair was loose, snarled around her head, her hands sharp, her bent fingers on the keys. When she finally heard me, she stood and turned; the long sleeves of the oxford shirt she wore, their cuffs unbuttoned, made it seem as if she had no hands.

"I thought you were with me," she said. "I didn't see you, didn't feel you."

"I was," I said.

"No," she said. "You didn't go where I went."

She spoke so fast it was hard to understand her. Her eyes wide, she swayed slightly, on her bare feet, as if attuned to the storm.

"I swam back," I said. "I looked, I waited as long as I could."

"It didn't happen to you? You didn't go under?"

She glanced away, toward the window; the waves were crashing, spraying across the end of her pier. And then she reached out, her hand appearing suddenly from the cuff of her shirt, and touched the side of my face. Her fingertips were rough

and cold. She held her hand there for a moment and then took it away.

"Are you all right?" I said.

She stood there shivering, her arms wrapped around herself until I climbed halfway up the ladder to the loft and pulled a blanket loose. I put it over her shoulders, helped her sit down on the couch.

"I was down below and there was no way back," she said. "It happened so fast. Sit down! What are you doing, standing there looking at me?"

I sat on the couch beside her; her trembling radiated along my left side. The room around us was the same as ever: the colored beach glass, gently rattling against the window; the piano and Mr. Zahn's table with the carved lions; the wooden bluebird perched on the wooden plane; the picture of the cabin and the forest fire, nailed to the wall.

"What day is it?" she said.

"Tuesday," I said. "Wednesday."

I had no idea what time it was. Somewhere between midnight and morning.

"Where was I?" She spoke this question as if she shared it, as if she wasn't only repeating what I'd asked. She turned her head quickly, glancing around the room. "I'm trying to say. I just made it back. It's impossible. I can't—" Her voice trailed off.

The cabin creaked around us, trying to hold itself against the wind.

"I was alone out there," I said. "I didn't know what to do. I searched as long as I could."

Without warning, she stood, crossed the room and opened

the door, stumbling out into the darkness, the door slapping the wall outside again and again.

I leapt after her—across the gravel driveway, under the trees, their branches thrown all around in the storm—and caught her by the arm, slowed her down.

"What are you doing?" I said. "Where are you going?"

"I don't know!" She was shouting, tilting her face close to my ear, her hair against my cheek. "I'm trying to tell you what happened. A fish, a blue fish flew past me, it was a bird in the water. I don't know!"

Finally I got her back to the cabin, the door closed against the wind. Then I had to go out and retrieve the blanket that she'd dropped on the driveway; when I returned, she was stretched out on the couch with her eyes closed. I spread the blanket over her; I looked down into her face, and she seemed older than she had before. And then her eyes suddenly opened, gazing up at me.

"I'm leaving soon," she said.

"Why?"

"In a few days. Maybe sooner?"

Her eyes closed again, and there was only the sound of the waves, the candles flickering in the draft. Her chest rose and fell, a slow rhythm; I believed she'd fallen asleep when suddenly she spoke again.

"I was hardly awake," she said, "but I wasn't asleep. I felt myself as a girl, walking along a path in the forest. I could hear the water nearby, but I couldn't see it; I felt myself in other times, other places, as if I were there. The bluebird swam into my hand and lay still, then flew away again."

"Okay," I said.

"And then I opened a door and the water rushed in and I swam up through it, to the surface, and I began swimming again."

The windows rattled, the wind gusting around the house; the candles flickered, guttered, stayed alight, shadows leaping and falling along the walls.

"A door?" I said. "What door?"

"It's impossible," she said.

"You could have drowned," I said, "and I didn't do anything. I just swam back here and didn't tell anyone that I lost you out there."

"But I didn't drown," she said.

"Still," I said.

"Don't worry," she said, closing her eyes. "I'll be fine. And you, you will also be fine. Now I need to sleep."

I stood there for a moment; I listened as the weather beset the cabin, the windows vibrating their own conversations. I imagined how it would be if the storm kept growing, accelerating—the shingles jerking up like black tongues, then slicing away, sharp through the air, the windows shattering.

Finally, when I could hear that Mrs. Abel was asleep, her soft breathing beneath the wind, between the crashing waves, I blew out the candles, turned down the lamp. I went out the door and started back through the woods toward the Red Cabin.

Out in the night, through the dark tree trunks, I could see the long rows of whitecaps on the lake, surging, climbing each other's backs, spending themselves against the shore.

- 20 -

Not so long ago, I swam out to Horseshoe Island, trying to remind myself of how it felt, long ago. I swam during the day, and I swam with my thirteen-year-old niece, Sophie, a swimming prodigy; my mother and my wife came along, paddling the canoe.

Sunlight spun and angled into the depths, bright in my eyes every time I turned my head to breathe. Below me, faint shadows, spinning rays of light; above and around me, the laughter and voices from the canoe. Nothing was the same.

On shore, my Aunt Dee had volunteered to look after my daughters. Dee lives in my grandparents' old house. It's now her house, up the beach from my parents' cabin. She's my mother's younger sister, and is a writer of books, too. She's an evangelical Christian writer, and while I was swimming to the island she wrote me this email:

> I'm so enjoying your precious precocious girls. I have learned so much!

I have learned that they must wear their seatbelts or their parents might lose them to another family, and many facts about the Boxcar Children.

I have learned that their mother wears black so as to not draw attention to herself.

I have learned that there is no God but that the world was created when two planets collided, and that the planets were created by aliens, and aliens were created by fairies.

I have learned that the rules in your house are that the gerbils cannot be let out of their cage and left alone, and that teasing is just plain mean.
. . . and so much more that even bribes will not release . . .

I responded:

Thank you so much! We have guinea pigs, not gerbils. And I'm glad the girls got all the details about the aliens and the fairies correct; that's what I'm teaching them . . .

- 21 -

The day after Mrs. Abel returned, I was down on our beach, trying to fix a wooden platform, a makeshift deck that my father had constructed years before. The waves had knocked the boards loose, pulled out the nails, and I was pounding the nails straight, trying to get all the boards back down, removing those that had gone too waterlogged and rotten.

The sky was overcast; low waves rolled in. All down the beach, piers and docks were taken in, sections stacked atop each other. I'd helped my father take ours apart—all except the one post he liked to leave, to hear neighbors' reports of how long it lasted, against the ice. Summer was almost over.

I looked up from where I was working—straightening bent, rusted nails, hammering them against a flat stone—and saw Mrs. Abel approaching, walking the shoreline from her house. She wore sunglasses, a floppy white hat. Had I ever seen her before, in the daylight?

"Looks like a project." She sat down beside me, watching me

work. Picking up a stone, she threw it toward the lake; it clattered down among the other stones.

"Thanks for listening to me last night," she said.

We sat there. I could see her hands, clasped together in front of her, and the ragged cuffs of that blue oxford shirt. Her feet in their beaded moccasins, stretched out in front of her. I wasn't sure what to say—I was trying to make sense of the previous night; it was frightening, exciting to me, how unhinged she'd seemed by whatever had happened.

"What if you hadn't come back?" I said. "If you drowned, and I had to always remember that?"

"I didn't drown." She turned her head to look at me, her face so close, then looked away again.

"I know that," I said.

"It's just hard to explain," she said. "Some of it I don't know how to tell." She paused, furrowed her brow. "I was swimming," she said, "you were there, and then I was standing on the shoal, walking on the rocks. And then all at once I felt a hole, with my feet, an opening. I slipped into it. But I told you this."

"You didn't," I said.

After a pause, she started again, her voice shaking, settling as she went: "I was scared, and I kicked myself up, toward the surface, where you were, and then I slipped down inside again. Into a space, a place where I could breathe. The water became so thick. And I couldn't feel my body, the edges of it. It was so dark. And I could tell there were rooms, but they weren't exactly rooms, and it felt so crowded."

"All this was under the water?"

"And there were other people there, I think. Not exactly. I

mean, yes, but not so I could see them or hear them but I wasn't alone at all, that's not how it felt."

"You said there was a bluebird that was also like a fish."

"There was."

Seagulls wheeled in the sky above the waves. They settled down the shore, hopped after each other, cried out with their terrible voices. Sitting there, I could feel our cabin, behind and above me, where my mother and father were probably looking down, watching, wondering what I could have to discuss with Mrs. Abel.

"Did I tell you I'm leaving tomorrow?" she said.

"You said 'soon.'"

"I have to go check on my parents," she said, "in Chicago, and then some other things, places."

A bent, rusty nail twisted away from my fingers, lost between the stones. I'd never really considered that Mrs. Abel had parents, a family somewhere.

"That's what I came to talk to you about," she said. "It's the Zahn house—I need someone to watch it, this winter." Her voice was formal, suddenly, as if she were already trying to move away from me.

"But you won't be here?"

"That's why I need someone," she said. "It's just a place to be, if you need a place to stay, if you don't have plans. If you wanted to write your stories, whatever."

"I can't tell what I want to do," I said, after a moment. "How long I'll stay."

She picked up another stone, threw it hard so it sliced through the air, splashed out in the shallows.

"I just wanted to do something for you. To help you out."

"I don't need help," I said. "I'll be all right."

She stood, then. She held out her hand; at first I thought she wanted to help me up, also, but then I realized she wanted me to shake. So I did. Her hand was cool, dry against mine.

"I'm glad you were here," she said. "I was lucky."

"Okay," I said.

"Okay, then," she said, turning away. "I'll see you."

I remember the sound of her voice, saying that, her last words to me that summer.

Just last week I heard from someone I haven't seen in almost thirty years—a girlfriend from high school in Utah; a woman I'd dreamed about, shortly before she wrote—and I responded:

> Maybe we should be told when we won't see someone
> for twenty years or more, or ever again? A simple alert
> from the sky?

- 22 -

My grandfather, my mother's father, was a handsome man, his gray hair swept back, wearing kelly-green golf slacks, blue Nike running shoes with orange swooshes. Or holding his monkey-headed cane with the ruby eyes, wearing a pale blue cardigan, reading glasses around his neck. Or on the badminton court, a racquet in his hand.

My mother was just here, visiting us in Oregon, and she brought a letter she'd found, that my grandfather had written to me. It was typewritten, and in response to a number of stories that I'd written, that I'd given him to read. It is dated March 17, 1992; here are some excerpts:

You show vivid imagination and a unique touch. You must keep at the job. Grandmother tells of the premier watercolor painter, Gerhard Miller of Sturgeon Bay: he went to New York to study under the best known teacher of the time, who advised him, "After you complete about a thousand pictures, you will pretty much know how."

I have few suggestions because I don't know enough. So far I miss the nurturing love interest—that's been paramount in my life. I need to feel more empathy with your characters.

To put things on paper has proliferating consequences.

- 23 -

I stayed alone in my parents' cabin, after they left for the winter. I swam every day through that September, even as the lake thickened toward ice. My swims became shorter and shorter; I tried not to shower or bathe except in the lake, and became progressively dirtier.

I wrote in a letter from that time:

On the calm days now, the big trout and salmon come into the shallows to spawn. The top of their tails and their backs stick above the surface and sometimes they rest their chins on the beach. I'm watching them, rest assured . . . The peninsula has really emptied out. It's desolate, though allegedly people will return to witness the "fall colors." We'll see. Eventually the cold will force me to move in some direction. Right now I'm not feeling too fiscally strong or confident in general, but that will change. The new novel is already starting to take my sleep and I hope to get to it some day.

In these letters, I wrote of a man I'd read about who took care of an abandoned baby calf and lifted it each day; by the time the calf had grown to a bull, the man was hugely strong, having progressed through those imperceptible increments. So I wished to heighten my resistance to cold.

I told everyone that I'd stay up on the peninsula until the cold drove me away. It's more honest to admit that when I left it was because I was lonely. This was at the very beginning of November.

THREE
—

- 24 -

That November of 1994, I returned to Salt Lake City, where I was born and raised. I moved back into my old room in the basement—my childhood toys still in the closet—and tried to write, and tried to interest girls from my high school whom I'd scarcely known.

Why would they be interested in me? Because I said I was a writer and had returned, in my midtwenties, to live in my parents' basement?

Eventually I moved to a tiny adobe house in Mount Pleasant, a little Mormon town founded by polygamists, dead center in the middle of Utah. The house was owned by a friend's mother, who had fixed it up. This generous woman, Ilauna, encouraged me; she told me I could stay there for free, as long as I wanted, to work on my writing.

I actually did write, in that adobe house. I started the first book I ever published, a story of a young Mormon girl who was dissatisfied with her faith, who desired miracles, and of the old man who tried to provide them for her, who lured her in.

The girl in that book was my hopeful projection onto the smart Mormon girls I'd known in high school—I believed that they must be dissatisfied, and that someone like me could be the answer. Neither one of these beliefs was true, but still I wrote letters to Salt Lake City, trying to lure these young women in, rushing to the mailbox each afternoon hoping for their infrequent, kind, not encouraging responses.

(Rilke, again: "I sometimes wonder whether longing can't radiate outward from someone so powerfully like a storm that nothing can come to him from the opposite direction.")

I sat long hours at a rickety card table with my notebooks, my stack of books. When I wrote, the table trembled. Sometimes its legs folded, suddenly, the whole thing collapsing away, leaving me with my pen in hand, stabbing at the air. I had recently marked the seriousness of my fiction by acquiring a fountain pen—a green Waterman, made in France, that I'd convinced my parents to buy for me. I liked to think of Richard Brautigan's *Trout Fishing in America*, where a character says that "a gold nib is very impressionable. After a while it takes on the personality of the writer. Nobody else can write with it. This pen becomes just like a person's shadow. It's the only pen to have. But be careful."

That pen lay forgotten in a drawer for years and years. I find it, take it apart; I lay the nib in a bowl of hot water. Slowly, reluctantly, the ink seeps out, holding itself separate from the water, collecting thick and black, bloodlike in the bottom of the bowl. I wanted to write this story using this pen, but the nib is too scratchy, attuned to the personality of someone I am no longer.

Instead I rest the green pen on my desk, as a reminder, right next to Mr. Zahn's bone-handled pocketknife.

Back then, as now, I wrote everything by hand, before I typed it on my computer. That old Toshiba laptop: I had to wedge a copy of the *Collected Sherlock Holmes* under the screen, so it would not flop over. Beneath the card table sat my printer, a dot-matrix Citizen 120D—as it printed, I'd watch with fascination as one pass of the platen brought a jumble of marks, and the second pass brought the missing pieces of the letters; words and sentences became whole.

- 25 -

I met a high school girlfriend, from Utah, and we shared a glass of water. That was all. Where were we? We were both extremely thirsty and kept passing the glass back and forth, drinking, but it remained full of water.

We met many nights later, in a house that her family sold long ago, and finally, in an upstairs bedroom, consummated our relationship. This is something that never happened in our waking lives.

Then, a year later, in another dream, she's working at a restaurant on a coast and I come to camp on the shore nearby. I tell her I want to be more to her than a visitor for a week, more than merely someone from her past, and she says "That's what you said last time." We're talking at my campsite but a friend of hers, another waitress, is there, so we're half-whispering and I'm uncomfortable because clearly the friend can hear all of this, and I have the slippery sense of embarrassment and failure—I know that this old girlfriend is referring to how poorly I behaved in the last dream, when we were reunited in her family's old house.

If a dream can actually be aware of and refer to a previous dream as a history, is there a continuity, another life, somewhere?

Or it's perhaps that I did not engage or resolve that waking relationship as I might have, that I was immature and hurtful, even without meaning to be, and so I must continue to live it again and again, to feel that sting of helplessness and shame at different stages in my life, to be reminded.

In these linked dreams, I seem to be almost fifty, my current age, and yet there's no sign or awareness that I'm married or have children, or of any experiences since high school, since my failure with this person. There are no impedances or obstructions, only the possibility to fail again, to be incapable of summoning the necessary bravery or emotions or maturity. I must experience, anew and repeatedly, the mistrust of this person from my past.

The painter Charles Burchfield calls dreams a "strange world that seems a memory of childhood's impressions partly, and partly something that I never have experienced. I have had many such lately; there is a glamour about them that makes them seem much more desirable than real life, an agonizing feeling that they represent a world that I can never hope to find."

In his journal from December 5, 1961, Burchfield recounts a dream of a picnic where his family inadvertently takes and eats the food a poor family had left in a stream, to keep it cold. Apologies and reparations are made, and all ends well.

"Dreams like the above are inconsequential," he writes. "But what puzzles me about them is that they contain situations which I never actually experienced or thought of, and people whom I never saw in my waking moments."

- 26 -

Alone, that winter, I often thought of Mrs. Abel. She was the last person I'd spent much time with—even if or because so much of that time was silent, out in that black, mesmeric water.

My neighbors in Mount Pleasant, whose houses weren't close, never came over to introduce themselves. However, I liked to believe that they were curious about me; I walked past their houses, slowly along the sidewalk-less, icy street to the supermarket, where I'd stand in the parking lot with the cold handset of the payphone against my face, calling my parents.

This was before cell phones, and before email, before the internet. I had no phone in that little adobe house. I wrote letters. I wrote to the girls in Salt Lake City, and to my ex-girlfriend, and long letters to Mrs. Abel.

Just last week, in my rummaging through these boxes, I found a 3.5-inch square diskette that had *BACK UP 1993–95?* written on it. I pulled the thin metal plate against its spring, looked at the black disc, there, burned with old matter.

It's been over ten years since I had a machine with a disk drive that could read that diskette. But I took it to the technology people at the college where I teach, and they unlocked it. Even though some files were damaged, and even if I had been writing with a word processor that no longer exists, they accessed this artifact:

February 11, 1995

Hello, hello,
I just realized that I don't think I've ever said your name to you, that there isn't a name that I call you. I can't remember if I ever heard you say my name. That's okay.

You can tell by the postmark that I am back in Utah. Where are you? I'll send this to Ephraim and hopefully they'll forward it.

I stayed there until November, only.

I am living here in a two-room adobe house with a bathtub and toilet in my bedroom, behind a screen. The postmistress told me that the house has two front doors because it was built for the wives of a polygamist. The threshold between the rooms is pock-marked and rounded by sheep's hooves because the house was used to shelter sheep for twenty years, before a friend of mine's mother fixed it up. I have a barn and a pasture and at the edge of the pasture are bare trees. In one of them is a huge tangle of sticks, an eagle's nest, though I haven't seen the eagles. Not yet.

The other day, I looked across the pasture and saw a

woman in a bonnet, in the driveway of a distant house, climbing into a pickup truck.

How are you? I am fine. I miss you, I think it's all right to say that. Days go by, here, where I don't talk to anyone, don't say a word. There's only one grocery store, no swimming pool. I miss swimming.

My only friend here is a big black dog that must belong to a neighbor. This dog chases the snowplows, up and down the street, the white waves they make. He has one crooked foreleg, so maybe he caught a plow, once. He watches me writing, here, his face at the window and his breath steaming it up. He's a very quiet dog. He never barks. If it's a really cold night, I let him inside.

I wish we were swimming. There are things now I want to ask you that I didn't (couldn't). I wonder what you are doing. Sometimes I think about what if I were in Mr. Zahn's house right now, up in Wisconsin in the winter, the way you asked me to. Would you have come and visited me? I don't know.

The other day I walked to the grocery store and the woman at the deli counter asked me about my dog. I turned around and there he was: silent, watching me, sitting in the aisle. The lady asked me if he was a seeing eye dog and I told her he wasn't even mine. But I got him out of the store, brought him back here to our street, wherever he belongs.

I thought you'd drowned. I was trying to stay close to you. I wish you could tell me more about what happened.

There's no one here. At the grocery store, all the shopping carts are frozen together. But the adobe walls of this house

are so thick that they hold the heat for days, even after the
fire is out.

 Here I forget what time it is. I lose pens, pencils, books,
scissors. The woman who owns the house told me that a ghost
lives here, and that the ghost is a little girl. I hope that this
is true. The other night I woke up and it felt like someone
had just touched the skin of my face and no one else was here.

The letter tapers off; it appears to be unfinished. Did I write more and, lacking bravery, delete some of it? Did I print it out and mail it?

- 27 -

In my files of potential story material from back then, there's a lot of information about the "psychic photographer" Ted Serios, a topic that has led me, over the last thirty years, to write many unsuccessful and abandoned stories. Serios possessed the ability of pointing a Polaroid camera at his own head and producing photographs of places he had never been or seen. He called these photos "thoughtographs," and claimed that his psychic abilities began around 1953 or 1954, when he allowed himself to be hypnotized by George Johannes, a fellow bellhop at Chicago's Conrad Hilton Hotel. "Mr. Serios is desirous of putting himself at the disposal of science," states an article in *Fate* magazine, "But he would like to get beyond the stage of perpetual demonstration and into more fruitful phases of investigation."

Ted Serios was noted by researchers for his sincerity; forty years old, he looked sixty ("Mr. Serios is a friendly, unassuming man . . . At least part of his health problem is in consequence of the strain of his mediumship and the isolation it has created through misunderstandings and skepticism"); he was a drinker, and one book I read mentioned, in passing, that he had been beaten up by someone wielding a two-by-four. When he took his thoughtographs he would typically get quite drunk; he would shout and wail and screw up his features. Some suspected these to be the classic tricks of a magician, distracting the audience, and many believed and believe that Serios was perpetrating a hoax. Still, he was never caught out, and he used a Polaroid camera, which removed the darkroom from the equation—the instantaneity made it more believable and immediate. "Present knowledge of the laws governing the physical universe," unnamed scientists concluded, "cannot explain this phenomenon."

The demonstrations of this phenomenon took place mostly in Chicago, in rooms without windows. Once, Serios promised a picture of a dinosaur in its natural habitat, only to generate an image of a giraffe on display in the Chicago Natural History Museum ("It will have been noted that Mr. Serios seldom knows in advance what is going to come out of the camera and that when he thinks he does he is often wrong"). He stared "fixedly" into the lens; sometimes the images would be all black, sometimes pure white. Buildings, airplanes. Often two figures, walking across a field or standing next to a body of water.

Serios's photographs, his thoughtographs—their blurred beauty suggests that something is being discovered, a haziness that belies an effort to turn the invisible visible. (Wittgenstein: "People often use tinted lenses in their eye-glasses in order to see clearly, but never cloudy lenses.") I press my face into these fuzzy images in exactly the same way as I once did with the photographs of Bigfoot, of the Loch Ness Monster.

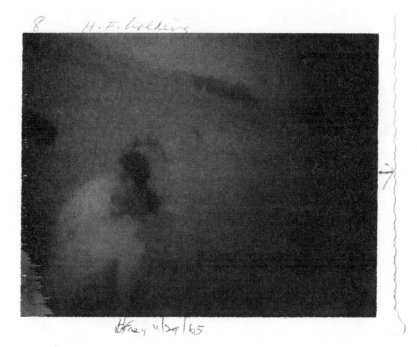

Experts said that the images of hotels were "often taken from angles and vantage points such as they could only have been taken from a helicopter." These are blurry pictures of tilting hotels, of columns and doorways, of women walking. Many images came out dark, shadowy, then in subsequent shots the shadows would coalesce into recognizable forms, as if surfacing from deep water. Sometimes the images would be of Serios's face, peering intently into the camera.

128

- 28 -

By myself in Mount Pleasant, I watched the windows, waited for the eagles. Once, during a storm, I stood in the rain and watched that nest blown apart, long sticks like spears falling around me. I looked out the window and thought: *If the next three cars that pass the house are blue or white, I will receive a letter today.* I decided: *If a bird flies higher than the barn in the next thirty seconds, there's really someone wonderful for me out there.*

My relationships had always devolved into silence and inertia and then I moved somewhere else, began a new relationship, stayed as long as there was still the faintest momentum from the beginning, that excitement of the unknown. My stories worked this way, too. Plenty of abrupt endings, doors slamming, trucks on highways. I was afraid to be still, to stay in a room with another person. I had no clue what people might say to each other, past a certain point.

In his book *Audition*, Michael Shurtleff writes, "I then ask, 'Why don't you run? What keeps you there?' The answer to these questions is what makes the actor able to function properly in the scene."

I could never answer those questions. I was continually searching for a scene in which I'd be able to function properly, rather than finding or recognizing or creating the reasons to stay.

Once, only a few years before Mount Pleasant, I'd lived with my girlfriend in Montana, in our little house with the pink kitchen; we had made our first attempt to live like adults, like people who wrote things. We built bookshelves, integrated our books. I made her a treasure hunt, for Valentine's Day, that led her through those books—a passage from Shelley on a scrap of paper led to *A Defense of Poetry*, inside of which was another scrap, from a quotation from Alice Munro; inside Munro, a note that led to Rilke, from Rilke to Wordsworth, Wordsworth to Flannery O'Connor.

One day soon after she moved west to be with me, she bought new running shoes and said she was going jogging; that surprised me, as she'd never been a particularly athletic person, and I also felt hurt, somehow, that she would rather run out into the frozen day than stay inside with me, where it was warm. I watched her lace her laces, then head out, awkward and ungainly, her sharp elbows jutting back and forth, her shoes so big, a brighter white than the snow.

She disappeared around the corner, leaving me behind, alone, and I wandered through our few rooms, looking at her things. Wedged between a dictionary and a one-volume encyclopedia, I found a spiral notebook that seemed to be her journal. I opened it, read a page, then slapped it shut, thrilled and ashamed of myself. She had written a list there, a series of self-recriminations.

1. A tendency to put on weight.
2. A need for always one more kiss than I'm given, another moment of affection.

What did I feel, reading that list? A kind of grim reassurance, I admit, that was not exactly sympathy and didn't change my behavior. I took it in as secret information I could hold and use, rather than conversations we could have.

- 29 -

Later that spring of 1995, I packed up my things and drove east in my blue pickup truck—out I-80 toward and through Rock Springs, then jogging up toward Casper, onto I-90, into South Dakota. These were names, places, highways I knew from driving back and forth with my family each summer, in our various station wagons, toward Wisconsin. I had never driven it alone.

I stopped only to buy gas or to piss on the shoulder of the highway—the truck still running, the door open, the light in the cab glowing out against nothing and the music blaring, slipping into the darkness. There was almost no one out there on those highways. I had to keep the music turned up loud, to stay awake, to keep my momentum.

I fumbled with cassette tapes, squinting to read the labels on the stickers; as I drove, I listened to Tom Waits sing, "Choppity-chop goes the ax in the woods, you gotta meet me by the fall-down tree"; I imagined this as a kind of soundtrack to what I was doing, some kind of film where my truck sped along the desolate highway and the camera zoomed in, gradually, closer and closer to me, the music growing louder until it was as loud as it was in the cab of my truck, where I would be staring out through the windshield with a resolute expression on my face.

I drank coffee, ate licorice, turned the song up louder. Sioux Falls and on into Minnesota. Rochester, La Crosse. I whispered along to the words of the song, and actually it wasn't that song at all, that can't be right—that album came out in 1999, years later. I was actually listening to "When the moon is a cold-chiseled dagger, sharp enough to draw blood from a stone" or "Someone's crying in the woods, someone's burying all his clothes. Roadkill has its seasons, just like anything. It's possums in the autumn, and it's farm cats in the spring."

The faint lights of towns, of cities—I imagined that children slept in those houses, and in their rooms, inside their warm beds as I passed, perhaps caught up in their dreams. There was no roadkill, there was nothing.

A thing, a fact that I was not thinking about, or trying not to be aware of, was that I had driven this highway, this route, less than three years before, and then I had not been alone. It was in the same truck, pulling a U-Haul trailer, and I was with my Canadian girlfriend. We had been leaving Montana and heading to New York, so she could begin graduate school. We would see what the future held for or would bring us, what quietly destructive things we would do to each other.

A month ago, a year after she'd first mentioned the letters to me, this girlfriend sent me an email; she told me she'd returned to Toronto, found the letters I'd written in our past, and mailed them to me. When I reminded her that I'd asked her *not* to send them, she told me that I could read or not read them, that I could copy them, but that she wanted me to return them to her.

Weeks passed, and the letters had not arrived. I wrote her back, asked if she'd sent them to me at home or at work. It turned out that she'd sent them to a house that my wife and I had sold years before; I don't even know where she'd found that address.

That house is only a couple miles from where we live now, so I got on my bike and rode over there.

My wife and I had been so happy in that house; it was the first house we owned, and we (mostly she) did so much work on it—the Murphy bed, the bathrooms, all that smooth linoleum. Since we moved out, we'd driven past on occasion, noting our curtains still in the windows, alarmed as the untended yard became overgrown.

And yet I had not been so close to it as that day a few weeks ago when I lay my bike down in the driveway, climbed the stairs onto the front porch that we'd had rebuilt. It was all so broken-down! Dish towels covering the windows, cracked paint, the stove dislodged from the kitchen, now on the front porch—I reached out and touched its chipped, white paint; in four years, I'd cooked so many meals, thousands of cups of coffee, on those burners.

It seemed somehow fitting that letters I'd written twenty years ago were sent to a place where I'd lived ten years before—not quite reaching me, only getting halfway back through time. Standing on the porch of that ruined house, so bleak, I felt that my wife and I had escaped another, bleaker destiny by moving away.

The letters were not there. No one would answer the door. I left a plaintive note, explaining who and where I was; I waylaid a postman; I even went to the station. Even my sister-in-law, Maggie, who knew a neighbor, got involved. I had wanted those letters, once, and then I had asked that they not be sent, and now I felt slightly bereft, responsible for their loss.

And then my wife and daughters and I flew to Utah for a week, to see my parents. While there, we visited the Homestead Crater, a mineral cone high in the mountains. Floating on our backs, in that warm water, we could see the blue sky through the round mouth of the cone, fifty feet above. Clouds drifted past. Voices echoed and came apart, dissipating up through that hole. My daughters were most excited by the dark figures of scuba divers, fifty feet below us. These bent, distended shapes rose, slowly taking the form of human bodies. As they surfaced, my girls swarmed close, delighted, shouting questions.

Yesterday, returned home from Utah, I was helping my daughters unpack from the trip when I glanced up, saw a movement through the beveled glass of our front door. I crossed the room, opened the door, and there was a package, sitting on the front porch. I heard a car's engine start on the street, someone driving away.

It was the lost package of letters. Torn at one end, furtively returned. I picked them up, brought them inside.

These letters were written in the last years before email—they were so *physical*. And there were other artifacts, too: photographs, and handwritten notes, and ID cards, all bound together.

Feeding the letters into a scanner days later, I read the post-marks, the times and places, the changing addresses; I imagined her opening each envelope, unfolding the pages covered with my handwriting.

- 30 -

[Autumn, 1990: Note written in Cross Campus Library]

[Excerpted letters, sent from Montana to New Haven, 1991]

January 27
*And I want you to see my little shack, my stove, where I'm
sitting while I write this, how you can sit in the outhouse with
the door open and look at the cows. You'll really know you're
here when you feel the cold seat of the outhouse.*

February 4
*When you said you didn't think you'd see me again it wasn't
just a terrible thing to say, it was wrong. Been thinking about
that time in the motel when I was on the phone with Byron
and you were out of the shower, walking around nude. I'd do
it again. Maybe a little differently. I want to do everyday
things with you.*

February 14
*I'm starting to get a better idea about how I want to write—if
I can get there, I don't know. Sometimes when it's late and
cold I piss out the window.*

April 17
*I'm glad you're better to me than you are in my dreams! You
hurt me all the time, but its ok. Just a little note to send
you this lamb's tail. It fell off yesterday. How are things there?*

April 19
*You're sadly mistaken if you think I don't have trouble falling
asleep; I was up half the night talking into my recorder,*

speaking what turns out this morning to be gibberish or another language.

April 21
I'll never tire of your scratchy letters. Come west, come west. Today I saw a strange, intriguing thing: all these heifers, running in a herd, chasing a jackrabbit across the pasture. It escaped through a fence.

April 26
It's surprising that the lamb's tail smelled—something must have happened to it.

This was the beginning of the relationship I was spinning out of, in that summer of 1994, when I met Mrs. Abel. Reading these letters, I try to understand this person, to become again the young man moving toward, preparing for mysteries he could not foresee. Encountering my voice from 1991, I feel a similar sense of the uncanny as I did that day in the Red Cabin. No person has ever felt more familiar and simultaneously so foreign.

(*Who was I, and what was wrong with me?*)

There I was, trying to convince my girlfriend to help me not be alone:

[Sent from Montana to New Haven, 1991]

July 31
I'm sitting on my steps and a sparrow's building a nest above me, dropping little pieces of mud.

August 27
Today a strand of barbed wire got loose and tore up my nose.

September 15
I want to live somewhere with a real table. What do you wish we could talk about that we can't because everything is not more ok?

September 19
You've written me a lot of nice letters and they help when I'm lonely. I especially like the one about us being cows with brushes on our tails, potentially hemmed in by cattle guards painted on the highway that wouldn't really grab our hooves. I hope we're not like those cows. I don't think so.

September 25
At this point, as far as writing I feel all I can do is talk tough. Meanwhile, the moon has been crazy, here, a big blue and orange hole rolling along the mountains.

October 8
I found a two-bedroom house in Livingston with a garage for $320 a month.

October 14
Sending two letters in one day is something that lovers do, I think. I'm going to get a book about how to make furniture. You do have very large and beautiful breasts; we have to find that shirt.

November 29

I don't know if I'd say you write coldly; with authority and confidence, poise: that is true. When I read this, as usual, I am left feeling that you can put your finger on it, where you want . . .

December 6

Yesterday I went and spent some time in the house and it tickled me even more. There's so much room—closets everywhere, drawers coming out of the wall in the bathroom. Amazing.

December 9

I even got new Montana plates for the truck, and a new driver's license. I seek authenticity.

When she finished college and moved out to Montana, we lived in the little house with the pink kitchen and worked our jobs—me on the ranch, she at the bowling alley, then waitressing at the Livingston Bar & Grille—and played house, and tried to write. To imagine places and people, to come up with all their names. She cut her hair short, and had a Carhartt jacket, like mine, that I'd given her. A fly-fishing cap, too, and heavy boots. It is sharply, tenderly embarrassing to imagine how we must have looked. Perhaps we dressed like this to suggest or create a similarity, a uniform, to convince ourselves that we were the same or to camouflage our differences.

One day in Livingston we were grocery shopping at John's IGA and in the checkout line we saw a little book of baby names and threw it down on the conveyor belt with our meat and broccoli and beer.

"Congratulations!" the cashier said, and we looked at each other obliviously, suddenly awkward.

"We're writers," my girlfriend said.

"Still," the cashier said. "That's great."

I said, "It's just that we have to make up so many names all the time, for our characters."

In that moment, did we feel the possibility that we might have a child together, children? I don't think I considered that possibility, consciously (*September 2, 1991: Last night I dreamed we (you) had three babies in rapid succession (within a couple days, though they were not triplets and were quite different ages). It all took place in a snowy/ice field landscape and I'd walk carrying the babies, changing their names. Naming was my job . . .*"); in any case, I know I wasn't ready, probably felt that we, she and I were not ready. I knew even then that we wouldn't have children together.

Still, I admired her, I admire her—the startling combination of her lisp that could make her seem so young and the incredibly smart things she said that made it all sound so wonderfully precocious. I remember a paper she wrote about John Ashbery ("It's this crazy weather we're having:/ Falling forward one minute, lying down the next . . ."); I remember holding its dot-matrixed pages in my hands and reading with envy and wonder the easy, conversational way of her intelligence: "There is no certainty that this poem is about weather as we typically understand it, yet its craziness is difficult to dispute."

———

These letters—an attempt to communicate with this one other person—are far better written and more interesting than any fiction I wrote, in those years. They are where I learned to write.

To read them describes, plots the points of a relationship—beginning, middle, end—in a way that is, in hindsight, almost comical, preordained. And to excerpt them as I have here is obviously to curate a certain narrative, to leave so much out, to present a self.

Yet I'm also aware of how often I made similar choices, back then; how I left things out when writing the letters themselves. I don't mention other infatuations or romantic possibilities. There's no mention of Mrs. Abel at all, even though (and this surprised me) the letters revealed that not only had I fled to Wisconsin from the end of a relationship that hadn't even quite ended, I had also, during that summer of Mrs. Abel, still been writing letters to the same girlfriend.

[Sent from Wisconsin to Toronto, 1994]

July 27
Just got off the phone and am troubled to hear you so troubled. I think as far as the move and everything you made the right choice and I'm sure it seems strange. I know (or hope) I'm cause for concern, too; I'm not sure what to say. I love you and I need to get some self-respect and impetus back. My flailing isn't your fault, of course, and it's not even that tragic . . . Anyway, meanwhile the rain is coming down again and my radishes are exploding upward.

August 10

I don't know if it's so much a need of yours to get things straight/talk things out as it's been you who does a lot of hard work and meanwhile I wait and let you.

August 20

(I have a great aunt who always writes two letters—one normal, the other apologizing for anything in the first one that could be misconstrued.)

August 31

It's hard to write—either it seems like I'm avoiding something by passing on news or I'm complicating an already complicated problem. I feel I'm letting you down by not being clear enough or not saying something I should have.

September 9

I'm not sure how I should explain my silence. I don't feel too silent, but then I don't have much to say. It's hard to write or talk on the phone because I'm self-conscious, in the sense of being conscious of presenting a self. You say you don't know me and you don't know what it's like to be me. Before when I wrote I said I was glad you knew me better than anyone and I believe that. I'm sorry I haven't been adequately able to say or even know how I feel, however I think that's what everyone's working on all the time. I'm not holding anything back! I always try to be honest, I try to be a good person. Sometimes that's not so easy to do. It hurts me to get some of your letters (like the one full of questions), it makes me feel insufficient and a little cornered. Yes, I get angry and relieved and lonely. All that's all right. Now's a hard time for us and I hope we can make it better than this.

FOUR

- 31 -

Whether thinking of or consciously not thinking of my old
girlfriend, I drove alone from Utah to Wisconsin, early in the
summer of 1995, the summer after the summer of Mrs. Abel,
about whom I *was* thinking.

I felt so strongly about her and I was uncertain of how I felt,
really, or exactly what had happened, the summer before; I
believed we might swim again, continue what we'd been doing—
that at least things between us would settle in a way that I could
understand.

My first night back, I walked down the beach to where the seg-
ments of Mrs. Abel's pier were stacked on the stones. The doors
to the space beneath her cabin were locked; I crept around to her
back porch and peeked in the windows, into darkness and shadows.

The door rattled when I tried the knob. It was only locked by
a hook and eye, and I went into the woods and broke off a twig,

then worked it through the gap between door and frame; I lifted the hook free, heard its tiny cold settling.

Inside, sheets covered the furniture, the piano. Yellow boxes of mouse poison were torn open, bait scattered across the floor.

I pulled the sheet from the table Mr. Zahn had made and kneeled down. Taking hold of the lions' wooden faces, I opened the drawers and secret compartments, all still empty except for the one that held Mr. Zahn's heavy pocketknife. I picked it up, pulled the stubborn blade open; cloudy, yet its edge still sharp. I folded it again, put it in my pocket, then closed the drawer, and covered the table with the sheet again.

She'd taken the carved airplane with the bluebird on it; the hook where it had hung pierced the air, sharp and empty beneath the loft. I stepped closer, I climbed up the ladder and peeked at the empty mattress, stripped bare, its striped ticking, the metal of its buttons worn through.

Out the window, the silent lake was the same color as the sky, the line between them impossible to see. Tacked next to the window, the same picture of the fire in the forest, the leaves tossed above those flames, the trees' branches alight. At the bottom of the slope, the little cabin with its one window. In the foreground, puddles of fire; overhead, a tilted crescent moon.

I took hold of that stiff, fragile sheet and pulled it loose, tearing a short line in the top margin, where the nail had been. Carefully, I folded the picture and put it in my back pocket.

- 32 -

One of the first things I did—that summer of 1995, before my parents arrived—was to ride my rattly old bike down to the post office.

I couldn't remember the name of the postmistress, but she knew who I was, and was surprised to see me.

"All your family's mail is forwarded," she said. "All to Utah, I believe."

"I know," I said. "That's not why I'm here."

"So how can I help you?"

"I was hoping you could give me someone's forwarding address."

"I can't," she said. "That's not something I can do."

"It's a friend," I said.

"If you give me a letter for someone, then I can forward it, but we don't give out addresses."

"This is for my neighbor," I said. "Claire Abel?"

"I'm sorry," the woman said, but she turned around, as if looking for something. And then she held a flat box in her hand. In it, I could see envelopes with my handwriting on them.

"She didn't leave a forwarding address. If I had one, I still couldn't tell you, though."

I stood uncertain whether to claim the letters, to say that they were mine and try to take them back, knowing also that I wanted Mrs. Abel to receive them, if she ever returned.

"So what happens," I said, "to the letters, then?"

"We hold them," the postmistress said. "Until she comes back for them."

"Did she ask you to hold them?"

"I'm sorry," she said. "Again, that's not something I can say."

"What if she never comes back for them?" I said. "Do you keep them forever?"

"I don't know," she said. "Could you step aside? There's people waiting behind you."

I rode away from the post office, up the slope and past the yellow SLOW BLIND CHILD sign. When we were young we always laughed at that sign, at this child, doubly afflicted; later, I saw a photograph of my brother's dorm room in college, where that sign, stolen, was proudly displayed. Still later, my friend Steve Sauter bought and moved into the house of the slow blind child, a house with a broken elevator that took Steve ten years to renovate.

I pedaled on; the bluff rose on my right and for a moment I imagined I was underwater, my legs pedaling in slow motion. Up another slope, through the intersection, I rode up onto Moravia Street where the trees' branches met like an arch overhead, the shade deep beneath them.

I passed the house and studio of the watercolor painter

Charles Peterson, who is well-known for painting ghost images, wherein benign spirits, past people, coexist in present times, sharing space with the living. The faded figure of a woman looking out a window, caught in the reflection of the glass; a seemingly empty rocking chair that, upon closer inspection, holds a mother reading to her child; an abandoned schoolhouse full of transparent students.

Peterson painted my portrait once, when I was ten years old. For some reason my parents had each of us—my two sisters, my brother and me—painted when we were ten years old. And these spectral portraits always hung in the living room in Salt Lake City, as if we are the same age, uneasy quadruplets—only now my parents have sold that house, dispersed its contents. The portrait of my younger self now hangs in this room, watching me while I write these words.

I look serious, uneasy, trying to hold my head steady, not to blink while I was being painted. (Shortly after my portrait was delivered from Wisconsin to Utah, it was discovered that someone (definitely my older sister) had penciled in my nostrils and it had to be sent back, repaired.) Also, I look hopeful.

- 33 -

No one had heard from or about Mrs. Abel, when or whether she planned to return. As the weeks stretched on into July, my hope for her return lapsed, and I reverted to my old ways. I drank beer at the AC Tap, ate innumerable bratwurst, and didn't swim much at all. I'd been granted a writing fellowship, in California, where I would move in September—that fact relieved any sense of responsibility or anxiety regarding what I should be doing.

A suspicion festered in me, however; I kept thinking about how Mrs. Abel had offered Mr. Zahn's house to me, how eager she'd seemed that I stay there.

I began to watch Mr. Zahn's house. I'd sneak up the cow path, climb into the old wooden fishing boat in the trees, the *Anne Marie*. From there I could see across the yard and into the lighted windows; I could see the dark shape of a young man as he moved from room to room, the blue flicker of his television inside that space.

He'd taken my place, stayed in the house all through the winter and was still living there. His name was Doug Plouff. I wondered about him, how well he knew Mrs. Abel, or if he'd merely answered an advertisement.

Years before, Doug and I had worked together, as dishwashers at the Carroll House Restaurant, but we'd not stayed in touch; he was a local, not a summer person. In the years since I'd known him, he'd lost one hand in a motorcycle accident, but was still washing dishes—at the Edgewater, that summer of 1995, where my younger sister was working as a waitress.

From inside the fishing boat, squinting across the yard, I could also see that the rooms were mostly empty, that all of Mr. Zahn's animals had been removed. Mrs. Abel had had them all moved, had hired people to carefully wrap everything, to put it all in storage. Back then, that made no sense to me, or anyone, but if you research Robert Zahn now you'll find him referred to as "The Birdman of Door County," and learn that his work is collected by experts, and in the collections of the Guggenheim, the American Folk Art Museum, and the Museum of Modern Art. I recently purchased a book about him; the preface says: "Folk artist? Outsider? Visionary? Vernacular artist? The labels point to a unique genre of art—art made by natively talented, untrained artists whose work contains a unique vision."

When I think of Mr. Zahn, what I remember is his open eyes, the knife in one hand and the half-carved bird in the other, the wood shavings on the floor and Mrs. Abel and myself, both alive, in that screen porch with him.

———

And now my daughter slides the door open, peers into this room.

"Daddy," she says, "if you die while you're having a dream, do you get to keep the dream?"

"Yes," I say.

I suppose that I could have befriended Doug Plouff again, managed to get into Mr. Zahn's house that way, yet that seemed more deceitful somehow, and I did not want to be inside if he was going to be there, watching me, asking questions.

One night I watched Doug—a weekend night, when I suspected he'd go out drinking (my sister had recounted some of the misadventures he'd told her about, out all night with a friend named Fat Pat). I waited until he came out of the house, climbed into his car (an old brown Pinto that had actually belonged to my family, once, that my father had sold him for two hundred dollars, that had no floorboards on the passenger side, so you'd be splashed by any puddle) and drove away.

I stole across the overgrown yard, lifted out a screen, and climbed in an open window.

Inside, there was a mattress on the floor covered in tangled sleeping bags. Two beach towels—one Packers, one Leinenkugel beer—were attached to one wall, like banners. A bean bag chair and a canvas camping chair faced two television screens—one large, one very small, both balanced on blue plastic milk cartons.

In the kitchen, beer cans, pizza boxes, a sink full of dirty dishes. I pulled out the drawers, and they were mostly empty. Plastic forks, tangles of rubber bands, fishing hooks. Nothing there—I spun around, searching, my eyes everywhere—felt how I remembered it; it didn't seem at all like the place where those wooden animals had been, crowded together, where the old man had lived.

I crossed out through the doorway to the screen porch and switched on the light: a metal folding chair, a cardboard box with an overflowing glass ashtray atop it, next to an orange bong covered in Kawasaki and Harley–Davidson stickers. I switched off the light and stood there, listening to the wind in the trees, looking out through the screens at the shadows in the branches, the darker blackness where the cow path descended along the cliff. This is where we'd been, a year before, and now I was the only one left.

Back in the main room, I dragged the bean bag chair to one side. I lifted one end of the mattress, as if that would help me. The lights were on; anyone outside could see me, whatever I was doing. Looking behind everything, under everything, lifting piles of paper and setting them down again.

It was then that I saw the lions. Up high, on the ends of the wooden beams that ran across the ceiling: two carved wooden lion heads, just the same as those on the table Mrs. Abel had taken. Quickly, I lifted the rickety canvas chair and set it under the ceiling beams. I climbed up, balancing, teetering, to see if the lions would somehow open.

At first, nothing, then I squeezed harder on the sides of the lion's jaws and it came off in my hand, revealing a space, a compartment, there. When I squinted, I could see a small handprint, pressed into the plaster. That was all.

I replaced the lion's head, leapt down, dragged the chair to the other side, almost tipped over as I reached upward. This one seemed stuck; at first it wouldn't move, but then all at once it did, and something flashed white, out at me—a bird? I flinched, closed my yes; when I opened them, it took a moment to find it, to see the yellowed paper, curled in a roll.

I leapt down, picked it up from the floor, opened it just enough to see writing, print from a typewriter. I didn't read it, not right there, but I somehow knew that this was it, what I'd been seeking. Carefully, I set the paper on the sill, then climbed back out the window, as if the house had no doors. I turned to close the window, and the paper was gone; I leaned my head back through the window—nothing on the floor—then stepped back. There, rolled out onto the ice, settled alongside the house. Tenderly, I snatched up the paper, rushed across the yard, back to the safety of the *Anne Marie*. Inside, holding the paper up in the moonlight, I began to read:

```
The Widower and the Girl Who Came From the Sea

There was once an old man who lived on the shore
of a vast sea. He spent his days training to spy
glass upon the waters.  One morning during a storm,
he saw a dark shape, far offshore.   Slowly, very
slowly it approached, arrived dix directly at where
the man stood holding his spyglass to his eye.
    It turned out that the shape was a kayak, and
inside that kayak was a young girl.   She was
silent and it took the old man a stretch of time to
```

teach her to speak   Even before she could speak, however, there were the incidents with the animals.

In some versions of this tale, the old man took the young girl as his wife. Most who tell the tale came from the land across the sea. Others say she was of an island people. Yet others claim she came from the sea itself, not from any land at all.   In many versions, the girl does not arrive by kayak, but is swimming and the man, sailing in a boat, intercepts her and thus saves her from the storm.

There were reports, after the young girl's arrival, that at night forest animals would call out in human voices.   And once the girl and the old man were walking along a a forest path where they encountered a poisonous snake.   T The girl told the old man to take off his jacket, pull it all inside out, and then put it back on.   Next she began to laugh a low-pitched laughter, then spoke two words that were unfamiliar to the old man, thatsounded to be in another tongue.   At this, the snake coiled tightly around itself, twisted into a knoxt, and died within moments.

In fact, the knot was so tight thatno man in the village was able to untie it, and so the dead snake was never straightened or properly me assured.

Another time, the girl pointed to a blue bird perched on a branch.   She clucked her tongue and the gird fell to the ground.   The girl picked it up, put it in the pocket of her dress and took it out again--

The bottom edge of the paper was torn away, right in the middle of that sentence.

- 34 -

Intrigued, frustrated, I wrote Mrs. Abel one last letter and delivered it to the post office, where it could wait for her, along with the others. It was a short letter, almost entirely questions; I wrote it at the table in the Red Cabin, then walked out under the trees, climbed onto my bicycle, and coasted down the hill into town with all those questions buzzing in me:

Is the girl in the story you?
How much more of it is there, or is that all?
Did you write it, or did someone else?
And why did you give it to me?
Where are you?

- 35 -

I read that fragment about the girl and the old man so many times that summer—alone in the Red Cabin, I'd furtively get it out, afraid that someone might interrupt me, ask me what I was reading or where I'd found it—that I almost memorized it.

I still have that scrap of paper, taped into a notebook with the piece of birch bark, the picture of the cabin and the fire in the forest. When I reread the story, now, it seems possible that it has nothing to do with Mrs. Abel, that she didn't put it there at all. Perhaps Mr. Zahn himself wrote it, hid it there when he built the house, a riddle for a child or grandchild to find.

When I reread the story now, I get caught up on one line:

There were reports, after the young girl's arrival, that at night forest animals would call out in human voices.

Perhaps this is because I'm in the process of reading *The Chronicles of Narnia* to my daughters, before they go to bed at night, sending them to sleep with all these tales of Talking Animals.

What I find most fascinating and disturbing are the accounts of Wild Animals that become Talking Animals, then relapse, or those awkward moments where it's unclear whether animals encountered are one or the other. For instance, on the last page of *The Horse and His Boy*, the mention of the "Lapsed Bear of Stormness, which was really a Talking Bear but had gone back to Wild Bear habits" before it was beaten so severely that it "couldn't see out of its eyes and become a reformed character."

The most troubling passage in these books happens in *Prince Caspian*, in a world where it's believed that Talking Animals are only a myth, when in fact they were nearly exterminated by the Telmarines, and are in hiding. Once Caspian has escaped his uncle and is on the run with the Pevensie children, they come across Talking Animals and travel with them through a wilderness where "wild, witless and dumb" animals also roam. Among the latter is a bear that they kill and eat, its flesh wrapped around apples and roasted over a fire. It's a complicated situation, this uncertainty, as they encounter new animals—difficult to know whether each new one is a friend, prepared to have a conversation, or a wild, witless and dumb beast, prepared to eat them or to be eaten.

Here's a conversation that the Pevensie sisters, Lucy and Susan, have, while that bear is being butchered by the boys:

"Wouldn't it be dreadful," Lucy said, "if some day, in our world, at home, men started going wild inside, like

168

the animals here, and still looked like men, so that you'd never know which were which?"

"We've got enough to bother about here and now in Narnia," says practical Susan, "without imagining things like that."

When I was a boy in Salt Lake City, my father read to me about the Talking Animals in *Narnia*, the talking rabbits of *Watership Down*. Hazel and Fiver, Bigwig and Buckthorn. At the end of a chapter, my father would stand, turn out the lights, and go out the door, closing it behind him. I'd listen to his footsteps, climbing the stairs; in that suddenly dark room I moved my feet to the warm spot on the mattress where he'd been sitting.

I spent a lot of time, back then, behind our garage, talking to my rabbit, Mercury. I believed that he would talk to me if I could only convince him to trust me; he would tell me secrets that no human could know.

At the same time, now, as I'm reading *The Chronicles of Narnia* to my daughters I am also reading Freud's "The Uncanny," a favorite from twenty years ago, a piece of writing that I still admire and find provocative. The passage that besets me concerns wax dummies and mechanical dolls, automatons; it also discusses how epileptic fits might suggest to one who witnesses them that there is something *mechanized* within the sufferer. This creates suspense, an uncertainty about whether a figure is a human being or not.

I think of what the excellent Mr. Beaver says, in that first book of *Narnia*: "But in general, take my advice, when you meet anything that's going to be human and isn't yet, or used to be human once and isn't now, you keep your eyes on it and feel for your hatchet."

Perhaps the most impossible insight might be to recognize that another person (or oneself) is actually a human being, or is becoming one. And then truly understanding and being certain of it—to set down your hatchet and summon the courage to pursue this belief, to investigate how that will be.

- 36 -

While I waited for my tank to be readied, I listened to a gray-haired adept, behind me, tell a woman about a pizza entrepreneur in Kauai who had spent thirty days in complete darkness and silence, not speaking a word.

Books were for sale, in the waiting area; among them, *How to Get High Without Drugs*, alongside a spectrum of different colored sunglasses, for harvesting the healing powers of different wavelengths (Red denotes a strong sexuality; Yellow generates positive and optimistic qualities; Indigo combines reason with intuition, discipline with creativity) and a "True Mirror" that reflected my image without reversing it, allowing me to finally see myself as others saw me. Did I seem friendlier, more authentic and empathetic, as the sign promised? I wasn't certain.

This was my first time, floating in an isolation tank. I'd come in hopes of being transported to the past, of experiencing a "very strange brain event" like the one my old girlfriend had described. Perhaps I would encounter her, or even Mrs. Abel, again.

The bearded young men who worked at this place spoke in soft, calm voices. One led me down a hallway, past doors with signs on them reading FLOAT IN PROGRESS and to my room; he explained how to proceed, then left me to disrobe, shower, enter the water and turn out the light.

I breathed, floating on my back in that darkness, that thick salty water that held me, that crept in to fill and seal my ears. I listened to my breathing, the organs settling in my body. Was that an engine, a car out on the street? Was it still sunny out there, bright? I could not see my hands, next to my head; I could hear them bend, straighten, feel the tremble of the water, and that blackness was almost the same as swimming in the lake at night, when I also could not see my hands but only heard them, their splash and slap and my inhale, the rush of wind and night water.

Silence.

I am suspended. It is clear that I have turned, that I am now hanging over an abyss, a void, looking down into it, levitating. I feel the feathers of my lungs, the twist of my intestines. My heartbeat—I almost fall asleep and my leg twitches, my arm twitches, gently the waves wrinkle and settle around me as I hang like this. My heartbeat, and when I squinch up my eye against an itch I hear the sound of my brain flexing, winding, I feel the synapses crackling, chains and chains and chains that I move incrementally through and I am gaining momentum suddenly traveling very close to the ground, the white beach that I know, every stone, I have no body and I move down low, like the ghost of an animal, a bird, across the green grass of the Reeves' lawn, under the weeping willow, out into the woods, beneath the cedars, the ground orange and green and brown.

But I am not staying in Wisconsin, not traveling to that summer.

I know where I am now, by the light. I am in the time between that summer of Mrs. Abel and now. A woman rises from the bed and crosses the room—strong, her body so balanced and poised, no concern for being watched, no self-consciousness. Her hair is long and dark, a snarl across her shoulders; she tucks it back and I see the side of her face. This is San Francisco, 1996, and the walls are all white. Light carpet, a mirror that doubles her now, showing the other side of her body. A white shelf, a black CD boom box; I can even read the titles of her few CDs: Neil Young, *Harvest Moon*; Cowboy Junkies, *Lay It Down*.

This woman is not yet my wife as she gets out of bed and crosses the room, stretching one bare arm, balancing on one foot. She pulls on the cord and the blind rises up, the whiteness of the fog cast in over her skin. She turns, smiling at me, and steps back toward the bed. In that glowing whiteness, there is no sound at all.

FIVE

—

- 37 -

A few years ago, I was writing a novel about a girl who grew up in the woods. Hidden, resourceful, she was eventually captured. People tried to help her become integrated into our world.

My novel arose out of actual events, something that happened not far from where I live. In the true story, the girl disappeared and never surfaced again; this bothered me so much that I decided to hypothesize about what had happened.

I came to realize that this girl would have to tell her own story, to convey her peculiar wonderment. I have never lived in the wilderness, never been a young girl, and yet I had to figure out ways to inhabit her, to find her voice inside my voice. I did simple things, like take semi-colons away from myself; I looked at the fragments of the actual story for clues, doorways through which I might enter.

After the girl's capture—in the actual story, and in the made-up story, both—psychologists administered the Thematic Apperception Test to her. This is a test in which the "procedure is that of merely presenting a series of pictures to a subject and encouraging him to tell stories about them, invented on the spur of the moment . . . As a rule, the subject leaves the test happily unaware that he has presented the psychologists with what amounts to an x-ray picture of his inner self."

I acquired a copy of the Thematic Apperception Test, a blue box (printed upon it: *This test is sold on the understanding that the plats are not to be displayed <u>and may be purchased only by authorized persons</u>*) filled with thirty-one pictures that range from a man climbing a rope to a child in a doorway to a woman on a bridge with the sun's rays cutting down all around her.

Using this test, an unauthorized person, I tried to make up stories as this captured girl might. As a way to get to know her, to reveal her character, to become her. The image that taught me most was a picture of a small cabin beset by a winter storm; in the Test's appendix it is described as "a weird picture of cloud formations overhanging a snow-covered cabin in the country."

In fact, the name of this painting is "The Night Wind," and it was painted by Charles Burchfield. In his journal, he reflects on it: "To a child sitting cozily at home. The roar of the wind outside fills his mind with various strange phantoms and monsters flying over the land."

And so I began to pursue Burchfield, after finding him in my pursuit of the captured girl. It was only then, turning the pages of a heavy book of his paintings, that I came across the fire in the forest and the cabin with its lighted window. Only then, almost twenty years after tearing it from the wall of Mrs. Abel's cabin, did I know the name of the person who painted it.

———

One afternoon in that summer of Mrs. Abel, my father asked me to sit down on a stump in the garden, where he was picking radishes, to talk with him. He said he had something important to say to me.

He was kneeling, the sun shining down behind the cabin. He wore a broad-brimmed hat, his face in shadow, a red bandana around his neck. Bees zipped around us; a pine snake slipped away, under the low stone wall. I sat there anxiously, waiting for him to speak, uncertain if he was going to comment on something I had done or had not been doing. Had he been watching me more closely than it seemed?

"In your life," my father said, speaking with great earnestness, "one of the greatest pleasures, one of the most important uses of time is to daydream."

It is fitting that Charles Burchfield's work should be found in the Thematic Apperception Test, housed in that blue box that is used to unlock a person, to allow a person's storytelling to reveal him in ways that he cannot control or otherwise articulate. "The test recognizes," its instructions explain, "that these fantasies and dreams are not less real than 'actual overt deeds,' and often more revelatory. What we hope and imagine and daydream is as real a part of our life, if invisible, than any action or conversation or outside appearance."

"In writing a diary," Burchfield notes, in 1911, "I first thought that only events should be written; then gradually I began to put descriptions in which led me to describe my feelings at seeing different scenes and objects; now I think I ought to put in my imaginings, for they are part of a person's life."

Charles Burchfield died in 1967, the same year I was born. He moves, resonates with me for many reasons, one of them being that in middle age he looked back at the work of his youth, more than thirty years before, and realized that he'd forgotten something, that he'd left something vital behind. As he writes in his journal on February 3, 1945: "A painting I destroyed at the time, which I now wish I had for reconstruction, was one of a blizzard in the woods. How little faith I had in what I was attempting at the time! How could I know that many years later I could complete these fumbling attempts at the impossible?" He added sheets of paper (he worked in watercolor) to his early paintings and expanded them, turning them into new compositions. As if he knew that he needed the energy, the blind boldness of youth, and now could couple it with the perspective and skills to match these earlier visions.

More than anything, Burchfield was a painter of weather: "For me, let me have a wild ragged sky, an icy wind, and some snow, and I am content."

Sound is visible, in his paintings—the rising, bent lines of crickets calling, the hooked electrical song of power lines and the telephone lines, voices trembling in the air, shaking the countryside. His houses look slightly like people, warped by the rain and weather; winds have eyes, the jagged suggestions of faces ("Why is it that I cannot seem to express the feeling on a windy day? The wind catches our mind, tears it loose from us and carries it far and wide. It is a feeling of supreme elation, of detachment from ordinary affairs").

Burchfield drew motifs, pencil drawings of spirals, curves, shaded curlicues that signified (and generated?) emotions. These he called "Conventions for Abstract Thoughts"—"Aimless brooding," "Fear of Loneliness," "Aimless Abstraction (Hypnotic Intensity)," "Morbid Brooding," "Melancholy/Meditation/ Memory of pleasant things that are perhaps gone forever"—and would disguise these symbolic pictographs as shadows in a steeple, the glare of a doorknob, clothing tossed over the back of a chair, to fix emotions in his paintings, to cast an atmosphere outward.

In World War II, Burchfield served in a unit where he taught camouflage painting. His main occupation, before devoting himself to his art, was as a wallpaper designer. And what purpose does wallpaper serve, if not to cast a mood or emotion into a room, to provide an atmosphere in which it becomes possible that things might happen?

- 38 -

Sometimes the phone rings, and when I pick it up no one is there. When this happens, even after all these years, I often think of Mrs. Abel; might it be her, listening silently on the other end? This, despite the fact that we never once spoke to each other on the telephone.

- 39 -

One March morning, only months ago, I made breakfast for my daughters and walked them to school (my eldest held my hand so she could continue to read *Ramona and Her Father* as she walked), then rode my bike through the rainy streets of my neighborhood to swim laps in the pool; later, I sat alone in a gallery, gazing into photographs, colors all around me.

In the afternoon, I taught a class, trying to help the students with their writing, turning to and leaning on my own mistakes.

I checked my college mailbox before heading home: there, a pile of paper that I jammed into my pack, along with a copy of Shurtleff's *Audition*, forced on me by a Theatre major who was certain it would clarify to me what I'd been saying in class. The book had a note folded into it, a list of page numbers I must read, and a star next to the very short third chapter:

3

Consistency

Consistency is the death of good acting.

Riding my bike home, I coasted down a long hill, thinking about what I'd told the students that afternoon—I said, "Momentum is everything, in a narrative. If you've ever ridden a horse, you know that when they see a hill coming they speed up, right before they reach it, so they can get to the top without straining. So it is with information— exposition, reflection, description, digression—in your storytelling. Something has to happen, to be promised, enough tension and anticipation and expectation, that you and your reader can easily, happily get over these hills of context."

The explanation was clear enough, but, as usual, a simplification. There are all manner of horses, all sizes of hills.

At home, I opened a beer and, standing in the kitchen, pulled the papers from my pack. Amid the memos and junk mail was one hand-addressed envelope, which I opened. Inside, two pieces of paper—one just a scrap, torn along the top, the other whole.

            then she breathed on t the bluebird and
it startled to life, trembling there in her hand.
It flew out the window and over the treetops.

    Each morning, the girl told the man her dreams.

    "Listen," she said one morning, "I was lost, out
in a forest, and I came to a tall wooden tower,
with astaircases that climbed back and forth.
From its top I could see out across the sea, and
one boat sa iling upon it.   I watched as that boat
took down its sails and set anchor in the harbor of
an island.   I stripped off my clothes and leapt
into the sea! I swam to the boat and climbed
aboard.   The boat had a small cabin, a locked
wooden door, but I had the key and so I opened it.
Do you know what I found?"

    "Tell," the old man said.

    "Inside the cabin was nothing but darkness, a
staircase leading down into it. A metal, spiral
staircase that went down and down and down.
Above, behind me, the door closed.   I continued my
descent, despite the darkness.   I could not see my
feet and so I reached down carefully, tapping each
new step with my toe.

    At last, I saw a dim light below.   It grew
brighter as I descended.

    "At the bottom of the staircase there was
another door, and light shone through a peephole.
I leaned close to look through it, and I saw trees,
a green green forest.   When I opened the door,
you were there, waving to me, holding something in
your hands."

    "I was?" the old man said.

    "What wereyou doing there?"   The young girl
looked up at him without a trace of mischief or
disingenuousness.   "Were you holding the bluebird,
or was it something else?"

    Not long after this, the girl went missing.
And from that day to the day of his death, the old
man would often hear the crinkling of paper, in the
next xo room, and then he would hear sniffling;
when he went to check for the source of the sounds,
however, the room was always empty.

    Sometimes, upon returning to his house, he'd
find small, muddy footprints across the floor. He
ran from room to room.   No one was there.

I read the story through again, then carried it down to my basement room and found the old notebook I needed. There, folded between Burchfield's fire in the forest and the scrap of birch bark, was the first half of the story, the fragment that I'd found in Mr. Zahn's house. The paper was torn right at the place where the new fragment began:

> Another time, the girl pointed to a blue bird perched on a branch. She clucked her tongue and the bird fell to the ground. The girl picked it up, put it in the pocket of her dress and took it out again——
> then she breathed on t the bluebird and it startled to life, trembling there in her hand. It flew out the window and over the treetops.
> Each morning, the girl told the man her dreams.

Upstairs again, I found the envelope, fallen under the kitchen table. There was nothing else inside; no explanation, no note; no return address. Yet when I read the postmark—*Ephraim, WI 54211*—it was as if Mrs. Abel were calling to me.

- 40 -

I wrote to my Aunt Dee, who now lives on the peninsula year-round, in my grandparents' old house on the shore. I told her I might like to visit. She wrote back:

Good to hear from you. Would love pictures of the amazing new playhouse. Your wife is a woman of many talents! Burying Carrie and the squirrel Sally KQ. I can picture the scene and am sure you could write about it splendidly.

My book on The Song of Songs is due in three weeks! I don't know what is next and always have this anxiety which I shouldn't, because my identity is in Christ and not in writing, but I have this tendency to return to religion!

I am going to be gone next Friday for ten days if you

want to come and stay at my house and experience Door County winter. Yesterday was a big melt, but I doubt that spring is really around the corner!

Love to you and your great women!

Dee

- 41 -

In Milwaukee, I rented a car and began driving north. It was afternoon, icy and gray. On the passenger seat, books that had been my favorites, so long ago, that I still admire—Cortázar, Wittgenstein, Hemingway—along with the journals of Charles Burchfield, my grandfather's *Hollow Tree*, and Shurtleff's *Audition* ("Start with the question: What is my relationship to this other character in the scene I am about to do? Facts are never enough, although they will help you begin . . . You must go further, into the realm of the emotions").

I checked the dashboard clock and thought of my daughters—at their gymnastics and hip hop dance classes, two time zones away; I wondered if they missed me, if they were thinking of me. Their school was in session, but for me it was Spring Break. And so I'd set out on this trip, explaining to my wife that it was essential that I experience that peninsula in the winter, something I'd never done. Besides, I had research funds to spend.

My phone, plugged into the car's stereo, played music I'd first heard over twenty years before, that I favored during that summer of Mrs. Abel. I listened as Lucinda Williams sang and it was as if I were back in the Red Cabin with the rain lashing the slanted, tar-papered roof. The strings swelled; her voice ratcheted up:

> *I walked out in a field, the grass was high, it brushed against my legs*
> *I just stood and looked out at the open space and a farmhouse out a ways*
> *And I wondered about the people who lived in it*
> *And I wondered if they were happy and content.*

The music also took me back to my adobe house in Mount Pleasant, after that summer; there, I had been so lonely that I had raised loneliness to the highest of attributes, completely necessary if one were to do anything worthwhile, or become someone, to become world in oneself, to draw another person to you and have them not be disappointed.

I drifted back further, to the drive east with my ex-girlfriend, a hundred cassette tapes on the floorboards at our feet (*Again, I am not good enough to write about you,* I said in one of the letters. *I never did you justice when you were around and now you're so far away!*). I drove, just south of Green Bay, with Two Rivers and Manitowoc and Sheboygan behind me. An oncoming car's headlights blinded me for a moment, and then my vision returned.

This girlfriend wrote me not long ago, by email:
Don't worry. Your letters are safe, now; they're under my desk at home.

I responded:

I'm relieved. Though I've been remembering things, since I read them—like one time in Livingston when there was some kind of fair/circus in town and you got really wigged out at night that a clown was running alongside the house.

I have NO MEMORY of the clown. My memory is ridiculous—sometimes I think it's having kids that did it to me, that makes it impossible to remember. PLEASE elaborate.

Anyway, it was just early on when we'd moved into the house and there was some kind of traveling carnival that we decided not to attend, but then later, much later, you either couldn't sleep or had a bad dream and woke up quite upset and worried about the possibility of a clown or clowns being outside the window or running back and forth along the house. That's all I remember. I was thinking, "Whoa!" but was kind of excited, too, about this possibility, though you were quite beset and seriously distraught. Maybe, I wonder now, you weren't all the way awake? I don't really remember what we said or did the next morning, but I think things went back to normal. I do remember you being really upset about the clown thing, though. Sorry if I was not more understanding or sympathetic.

Wow I have no memory of that at all!! But thank you. Don't worry, if you wrote about us, and I read it, I'd probably think it was about someone who was not me. But now I am more like you were then I think. You'd be amazed how much true stuff I put in *Mad Men* without anyone noticing. Nothing much about you, though.

Nothing much?

You'd have to watch closely.

What did you mean "But now I am more like you were then I think."

Ha. I meant that at the time I was wilder, messier. I was full of lust and dissatisfaction and questions. I always had this image of fire consuming everything I tried to write. Like the break-fire from *Young Men and Fire*. Now I am better at working and discovering my work, I am more thoughtful and solitary, more open to the world and closed to myself.

Ah, it is me, now, who is more like you were then.

- 42 -

I stopped at a McDonald's in Sturgeon Bay to use the rest-
room, to drink a chocolate shake and eat a Filet-O-Fish. Sitting
under those fluorescent lights, after hours in the darkness, staring through the windshield, I felt exposed.

A group of teenagers was shouting, carrying on behind me;
there were old men drinking coffee, eating French fries; a young
couple was trying to quiet their baby.

I was only an hour or so away, now. I didn't know if it would be
better to show up in the middle of the night, to surprise Mrs. Abel
(would she be surprised?) or sleep somewhere, wait until morning.
I closed my eyes and I was swimming, slicing through the dark
water, and she was beside me, to the left, her pale arm, her sharp
white hand in the moonlight; and then, somehow, she was off to
the right, we had crossed without realizing it, come close without
touching. We were off again, silent in the night, finding a rhythm,
our arms moving in unison, disappearing beneath the surface, out
into the moonlight, then disappearing again.

Eyes open again, I returned to McDonald's. Hamburglar, Ronald McDonald, Grimace, Mayor McCheese—are there a weirder assortment of friends, anywhere? Around me, the people had all switched out. A new group of teenagers, a family of four, two old ladies with apple pies, both exclaiming about how hot they were.

It was then that I realized I'd been expecting Mrs. Abel to be as I remembered her, though twenty years had passed and she'd be in her sixties, beyond middle age.

I am now the same age as she was, that summer.

There were no other cars on the road. A sign flashed in my headlights. Distances to Egg Harbor, Fish Creek, Ephraim, Sister Bay. I was getting closer, drawing nearer. Stars fanned across the black sky.

At Jacksonport, I turned left onto County V, the last leg of my childhood journeys between Utah and Wisconsin. These same highways, traveling with my whole family in the station wagon, heading north up the peninsula with a soundtrack of Styx, Barry Manilow, Kansas, Billy Joel, KISS, and Foreigner.

The lake stretched out below me in the moonlight as I descended the hill south of Ephraim: so frozen white and foreign, no boats on it at all. I followed the road that curved along the wide harbor. I didn't see another car, another person. Wilson's, the ice cream place, was shuttered. No boats tied to the piers, and walls of snow drifted up along the docks at the yacht harbor, Anderson's Dock. All the posts, out on the docks, glowed white, thickened by layers of ice.

Our road had been narrowed, two widths of a snowplow's blade, drifts high on either side. I passed my grandparents' driveway with its new gray sign, BRESTIN, for my Aunt Dee. The driveway was plowed but I drove right past it.

The road wasn't plowed all the way to the end, since it turns from public to private just before our driveway. There, I got out, pulled on a parka and mittens, and began to walk, trying to stay on the corrugated snowmobile tracks, where the snow was less slippery.

The bamboo shades of the Red Cabin were down; behind them, I knew, were the bikes and the garden tools, the lawn-mower, the beach chairs. The snow was not so deep, under the trees, and softer. My footsteps made no sound. Past my parents' cabin; through the windows, the picnic table was visible, and the grill, all the lawn and deck furniture brought inside, stacked up high. Past the canoe and rowboat, stashed beneath the deck.

The lake was so silent, glowing, the moon almost full. I looked out past our raft, resting on the shore, to the long smooth stretch of ice, the dark shape of Horseshoe Island far away.

I stepped onto the ice, walking on water. I felt the cold air rising around me, a seeping, a frozen wind coming from below. Far away by Eagle Bluff, below the silhouette of the tower, ice shoves—places the wind and current had slid the plates across and crashed them against each other—rose up jagged on the horizon. I walked out farther, deeper. I imagined the raft's anchor below me, remembered the stories of settlers caught on ice floes, drifting from Egg Harbor to the Little Sister Islands, miles and miles.

When I turned, our shoreline looked different to me. Whiter, the houses shuttered and dark, but it was more that I was used to seeing them while swimming, from the level of the water. I kneeled down, my face close to the ice with its cold shining up, and then it all felt more familiar to me. Scrabbling to my feet, I kept on down the shoreline, closer. The Wests' place, the Phillips', the Zimdars'.

No candlelight flickered in the windows of Mrs. Abel's house. No smoke twisted from the chimney. No face looked out, watching my approach.

I climbed over the ice on shore, past where the pieces of her pier were stacked. The rough doors into the space beneath her house were locked, snow drifted against them. I took the padlock in my hand, felt its cold weight through my mitten as I shook it. And then I crawled up the icy slope along the side of her cabin, around to the back where all the snow was chewed up and frozen in ridges.

The footprints of boots, the prints of animals. The door was wide open.

I had no flashlight, only the lighted screen of my phone.

There were candles atop the piano, the windowsill; I walked around the room, touching each wick, as if they might be warm, recently extinguished. No. A thick layer of dust rested everywhere, the smell of mold and mice, snow blown across the floor.

The table from Mr. Zahn's house, with the carved lions, was not there.

In the kitchen, I jerked open cupboards and slapped them shut, yanked at drawers so their contents spilled onto the floor—matchbooks, more mousetraps, pencils, decks of cards.

Back in the main room, I lit one candle, then another. I rolled the dusty rug aside, I unlocked the trap door and lifted it open. The darkness seeped upward, into the room. I descended into that cold blackness; once I was there, gently slapping along the walls, my eyes gradually adjusting as light filtered down, I had no idea what I hoped to find. The snorkels and fins and masks were all gone, the nails and hooks empty.

I climbed back up, lowered the trap door, locked it, and rolled the rug back over the top. Then I went up the ladder, into the sleeping loft, shone the light of my phone into that empty space—the mattress torn along one end by mice, bare springs catching the candlelight. Crawling upward, I lay down on the mattress, pulled a dusty old blanket around me.

I rested there with my eyes closed and felt the silence, pressing on me from every direction. The frozen waves, the forests of trees standing tall and cold, the empty rooms of the cabins along the shore, the ice stretching to the islands and beyond.

- 43 -

That summer, swimming: out to Horseshoe Island, around it; we followed the curve of Nicolet Bay and further south, through all the dark boats moored offshore of Fish Creek. Pirate Island, Adventure Island, Little Strawberry. My body has never been able to go further than it could, that summer. The flat black water, the moonlight, the waves and weather, the edges of storms. Below, around, invisible: the smallmouth bass, the perch, the carp and catfish and bullhead, the trout, the whitefish. The sturgeon hovering even deeper, perhaps, straight out of the Pleistocene with their shovel noses, their smooth skin, not a bone in their body, all cartilage, and their bodies longer than mine, stretched out as I was, swimming across the surface above them, swimming with Mrs. Abel.

North, past Little Sister and Sister Bay, then the Sister Islands. We swam distances through the darkness while everyone onshore slept in their houses. The two of us swam and the lakebed rose and fell beneath us, the currents and stars all around us. She swam ahead, and I tried to keep up, and I did not wish to be left behind.

Part of my pleasure of swimming in open water, especially at night, is that it makes me afraid. It frightens me. The unknown depths beneath me, the black current and all its dwellers, its undiscovered creatures. Swimming, I envisioned serpents, and I wondered about the St. Lawrence Seaway, whether a whale might slip through, might evolve to breathe fresh water.

Just the other day, I was walking through the playroom, where my daughters have various hammocks and trapezes suspended by chains. My eight-year-old, Ida, was sitting on a small, round trampoline, reading a book I'd never seen before, *The Mysterious Monsters of Loch Ness*.

"I think it actually lives there," she said. "There is proof, but there's not much of it. The problem is that there's more people that don't believe than people that do. And this book is old, so they've probably found out more since then."

When my older daughter went upstairs to play with her sister, I picked up the book: here in these pages, the old, familiar photos, the hypotheses (the Loch Ness Monster could either be descendants of the Plesiosaurs or else they must be some totally unknown creature) and appeals to reason ("In the twenties a scientist said he had seen a carcass of a recently dead Coelacanth and received scorn very similar to that placed upon Nessie witnesses") and the propositions: "The more you study the Loch and the case for its animals being real, the more real they seem.

This seems to be true of most phenomena that are eventually understood, whereas the further you investigate a myth, the less real it becomes."

I have always had an affinity with ghosts, lingering from the past as they do, unfinished with what they left behind. That said, the three mysteries that obsessed me throughout my childhood were UFOs, Bigfoot, and the Loch Ness Monster. I believed; I wanted to believe; I lay awake, trembling at the possibilities, taut with fear and excitement. I collected magazines with titles like *UFOs: No Hoax* and *Cryptozoology*, clipped out photographs and articles, kept them all in file folders, to display and convince. One reason I preferred the Loch Ness Monster was because it lived in Scotland and was safely bounded by water, unable to burst into my life, into my nighttime bedroom, as aliens or Bigfoot might.

Once, in fourth grade, I gave a presentation on these topics.

A smart classmate, Jennifer Durham, sharply questioned my assertion that an organism as large as a dinosaur could survive by eating nothing but the skin of its teeth. I found my source and quoted the scientist: "If the creature has been able to survive, it is only by the skin of its teeth."

That was an early lesson for me in the dangers of language, of reading metaphors literally and not recognizing figuration. This is a practice, a tendency that continues to trouble me.

- 44 -

I descended from Mrs. Abel's loft; I locked the door behind me as best I could, then returned through the woods, which was more difficult and took longer than walking on the lake. The wind gusted, and icicles chimed together, breaking off to knife down silently into the snow around me.

By the time I reached the rental car, my feet were numb, my jeans covered in ice to the knee. The sky was darker in the trees, away from the glow of the lake.

The cow path up to the bluff was drifted in, impassable, so I drove around—up our road then onto the highway, doubling back on the road above.

There was no sign to Mr. Zahn's place, but I knew which driveway it was, and it was drifted in, unplowed. I parked on the road, walked toward the house. As I came around the trees, however, there was nothing but an open field of snow in the moonlight, glowing faintly blue. There was no wreckage, no marks where the foundation had been—the house had disappeared, and everything was so silent.

I walked out into the field, across the glowing snow, into the space where that living room had been. I walked the perimeter of the house, tamping down the snow where the walls had rested.

I floundered, then, through the deep snow, to the edge of the trees. Under them, there was no boat. I kicked at the frozen ground until finally I dislodged some boards with faded paint on them, the wood all perforated with the teeth-marks of porcupines.

The cold moon shone down. The tires of the rental car spun, caught, and I drove back toward our road, through the trees, where my Aunt Dee's house stretched dark against the lake.

Long and narrow, the house has been expanded since my grandparents' time; it has windows on both sides, and I could see straight through it, the haunting white of the ice.

I found the hidden key, unlocked the door, then gathered my few things and carried them inside. I switched on the lights, turned on the heat, and kicked off my frozen boots.

The floor in the entryway was green slate, as it's always been. On the walls, photographs of Dee's grandchildren, and her children, my cousins, and even one or two of me—standing in shallow water, wearing a diaper, laughing or shouting. A note on the table welcomed me, explained how to use the complicated espresso machine, told me the password for the internet. I glanced up, across the sunken living room with its shag carpet; above the piano, a painting of my mother with Dee and their older sister, Sally, from sixty years before, when they were girls.

In the dark kitchen, I drank a glass of water, looking out at the ice, white beneath the moon. And then shadows shifted—a movement on the beach, through the sparse trees. I leaned forward, my forehead against the glass of the window. A shadow, a dark shape, hidden behind the tree. I hurried out of the kitchen, around the table. I unlocked the door, stepped out into the snow in my stocking feet.

"Who's there?" I called.

A scrabbling of stones on the beach, a crashing into the underbrush. A tangle of dark limbs resolved itself into the shape of a deer just as it bounded away.

Back inside, I found my computer, opened it, turned it on, and connected myself to the rest of the world. Emails from students about setbacks they were suffering, messages from colleagues about upcoming meetings, another from my wife about a hike she and our daughters had taken, a story about the girls disappearing deep into a cave, and a picture of a note they found inside a hollowed out tree trunk:

ghosts are dead people who's spirits haunt the place where they died. ghosts can be both good and bad. It is possibowl to walk thrugh a ghost

I took off my coat; the house was warming up.

Searching the web, it didn't take me long to find out what had happened to Mr. Zahn's house. I suspected that it had merely been demolished, making way for a wealthy Chicagoan's summer castle, but in fact it was being moved, relocated. A museum in Minnesota had purchased the house and had carefully taken it apart, piece by piece. They planned to reconstruct it exactly as it had been, to gather his far-flung carved animals and to repopulate those rooms.

Next, I carried my things down the short hallway, past the laundry room where we used to steal warm Fresca, where the badminton rackets were always kept. In the room where my grandfather once slept, blankets were piled high and thick on the single bed. I undressed and slid in beneath them. I closed my eyes and thought of Mr. Zahn's house, the pieces of it all stacked somewhere, waiting to be put back together. I wondered about the museum workers, and I doubted they'd know about the secret compartments, that they'd understand where to press so those lions' jaws would open. When the house is put back together I'll go to that museum; I'll wait until the security guard is distracted, and I'll climb up and open that lion. I'll see if there's a message or story inside, waiting for me.

I switched on the bedside lamp and began to read *The Hollow Tree*, aware that my grandfather—wearing a cardigan sweater, golf slacks, maybe smoking a pipe—might have, years before, written the words in the very room where I was reading them.

He jumps from Montaigne (patron saint of all digressers), to Darwin, to something my mother said when she was five, to Spinoza, and then writes, "One thing that has always fascinated me is how big (in feet and inches, in pounds or stone) were the people I read and read about in history? What did they look like and act like precisely? Their biographies sometimes give some general specifications, usually not."

His attention drifts in currents, crosscurrents, undercurrents. On the next page: "I've read many definitions of Zen. Here is a new one, 'Merely becoming what we already are from the beginning.' Below this in my journal is 'The map is not the territory.' That also sounds as if it means something."

For two days I asked everyone I talked to—at the post office, the Piggly Wiggly, the AC Tap—but no one had any news of Mrs. Abel. If anyone asked me why I was looking for her, I told them the truth: that I believed she was looking for me.

And if I do an internet search for Claire Abel, I find nothing, no helpful results at all. Even if I pay the search engines (as I have: PeopleFinder, anywho.com, Intelius, etc.), I only get people who share her name, who are not her age, who have children and spouses she could not have, who live in places she could not possibly be.

SIX

- 45 -

On January 7, 1934, Charles Burchfield writes in his journal: "Since then, the strange abstract dream-quality of this Storm over the Lake has remained with me as some remnant out of my boyhood, when natural events loomed larger than they do now. Perhaps it is even some vague memory from my first years of life at Ashtabula, some storm perhaps that made an impression on my infant mind, forgotten till now it turns up in a dream. For I believe that an impression once received, whether consciously or unconsciously, never leaves the mind."

When I first read about the psychic photographer Ted Serios, I was in high school. I found the mystery so attractive; I was drawn to the inexplicability of how a man might cast something (even or especially if he couldn't be certain what it was) from inside himself and into a camera, onto film: to make it visible outside himself.

A related and deeper attraction (and one reason the images Serios made continue to haunt me) is the promise this suggests: that what is lost and hidden inside us might be projected outward and surprise us. This lost and hidden matter waits for us, available, hoping to surface, to be summoned, if we can only learn how.

I feel the presence of what the person or persons before me had left behind, in this tight space, in this salty soup that holds me. Shadowy figures, shards of other times, glimpses into thickets of trees, rooms of houses I've never been inside; I begin to think of the actual people in the tanks around me—so close, just on the other side of the wall, suspended naked between sleep and wakefulness—and how their memories and fears and lives are seeping and bleeding into my own, sliding through the darkness, that in-between space.

Mrs. Abel's strokes, always so calm, in rhythm, the water blackly slipping around her. I've never seen a swimmer disturb the surface of the water less than she did.

I imagine her swimming across Death's Door, those miles between the tip of the peninsula and Washington Island where so many ships went down; when I envision how she held her breath and swam down through their rusted, broken husks, it reminds me of a Hemingway story, "After the Storm," and a passage I copied from it, that summer:

I took off my clothes and stood and took a couple deep breaths
and dove over off the stern with the wrench in my hand and
swam down. I could hold on for a second to the edge of the
porthole and I could see in and there was a woman inside
with her hair floating all out. I could see her floating plain
and I hit the glass with the wrench hard and I heard the noise
clink but it wouldn't break and I had to come up.

The long hair floating in the aquatic wind—that's what
attracted me, stayed inside me. Or was it the inability to reach
the underwater woman?

- 46 -

I moved to California, after that summer of 1995, to work on my writing in the company of other people. It surprised me to find, in the packet of letters she sent me, that I'd continued to write to my old girlfriend during this time. Still reporting on my daily life, sending stories for her to read, needing her reassurance and intelligence, trying to maintain her interest in me.

[Sent from Palo Alto to Toronto, 1995]

September 9
Been missing you, unpacking things (like this) that have been in boxes for a year and a half or whatever. Yes! I have a new home . . . My days of searching were desperate, hopeless, not even close . . . I don't have a real stove and my shower's in the kitchen, but I can get with it.

October 1

It is nice in Palo Alto, almost too nice. It's hard to know where the campus ends and the city begins; everywhere people are sitting at tables outside, eating bagels and drinking espresso. Also I saw some people walking around naked on the campus, very free and Californian. Sounds to me like you're a success. Took one of your iron pills (packed with the spices), so perhaps I'll follow suit.

When I met my wife, I lived in Palo Alto and she lived in San Francisco, an hour away. She had a job in a neurobiology laboratory, running tests on frogs, and I could not see her as often as I desired. I wanted to see her every day, all the time. I'd sometimes drive to her apartment and wait for her to return from work. (She'd given me a key!) I'd climb out the window of her apartment, up the ladder to the rooftop of her building; from there, I could see the swaying eucalyptuses of Golden Gate Park, twined with fog. I squinted out toward the ocean, over the rooftops, and felt that weather inside me where suddenly everything was possible. I knew that I had never felt this way about anyone, and that this might be my last chance to learn to be with another person, to not be alone.

Those days I would walk into Golden Gate Park, surrounded by others on the green grass above the playground, the Carousel. Down below, homeless people with dogs at the end of ropes walked past, pieces of bicycles in their hands; they clustered, they disappeared into the bushes and eucalyptus trees. And one man I recognized—about my age, always shirtless, wearing long tattered shorts. He shouted from the base of the hill, unhinged and beset. "Super girl! Where you at?" Bending down, he turned and looked through his legs at all of us, sitting on the hill, his face upside down and watching us, slapping his ass in time as he shouted: "Su-per Girl! Where you at, Super Girl? I love you, I love you, I love you! Su-per Girl!"

Email, back then, was something one might access at school, or at work. It wasn't something anyone had at home. No one had cell phones, either. People were more difficult to locate, to reach.

I wrote her letters, this woman who would become my wife; I wrote her stories, in fact, of one or two pages. They were more autobiographical than anything I'd written—a way to introduce myself, to share impressive facts about my past and, by also sharing less impressive ones, to demonstrate how comfortable I was, exposing my weaknesses to her. I wrote about my family, and working on the ranch in Montana, about eccentric people I'd known. When I read through these stories now I remember things I've forgotten, and notice omissions. I see how I wanted my wife to understand my past, and me. In these stories I'm a dreamer with unlikely skills, a romantic who had been preparing for her, who had been traveling toward her for years and years. That's actually how I felt, how I feel. But in these pages I'm also a person who never knew romance, never had other girlfriends, never had much to do with women at all.

It would be simpler, clearer to focus on where I am now, and with whom, not returning to those mysteries and confusions—those times, places, and people that I've avoided talking or even thinking about for so long, that I've hidden away, that I've evaded. And yet to avoid, to forget is a kind of betrayal, pretending that there's no continuity between myself then and now. I feel both ways.

In these stories I sent my wife (before she was my wife) I wrote about being a security guard in the art museum where I was not allowed to touch anything or talk to anyone, where I was forbidden to sit down or write anything, where I always felt so encouraged to turn the corner and see Giacometti's "Walking Man." I wrote about how I sank deep into pictures and paintings, how I furtively took notes, circling the galleries, how I held as many stories in my mind as I could.

Yet I did not mention how I'd walk down the long hill from the museum, after work, to the tall house where I lived, and how I lived on the fourth floor with my girlfriend.

Just the other day, I walked down that hill while I was floating in an isolation tank twenty years later, and I walked to that tall house and went around to the side porch, where the mailbox was; inside the mailbox were envelopes addressed to me, in my own handwriting. I opened them, standing there in the fallen snow. They were rejection letters from magazines that didn't like or "couldn't find a place for" the stories I'd sent them.

The letters I wrote, that my old girlfriend sent me, came bundled in a black ribbon that she often wore in her hair. It seems fitting that the last letter in the bundle begins this way:

[Sent from Palo Alto to Toronto, 1997]

June 4

Hello! Hope this finds you well. I should have been in touch before now; I've been pretty scattered, and things are not really settling, even now. What's up?

You may have heard that I'm getting married. That's true. It's still a little shocking and hard to visualize. A strange kind of levitation. It kind of overwhelms or puts into perspective everything else.

Not so long ago, my ex-girlfriend wrote to say,

> I also have come to a place where I want to be direct with people, where I am (finally! At this age!) trying to be in the world as I am inside, where I have finally noticed that telling the truth and being vulnerable and not knowing are not as frightening as I have always thought.

She told me she thought I'd like a talk she'd recently given at Cornell, about the ineffable in writing; this morning, sitting here in my basement, I watched it on YouTube. There she was, tiny on my laptop screen, wearing a red shirt, her voice I hadn't heard for so long, her hands out in front of her, gesturing with enthusiasm as they always had.

The talk was titled "Telling Secrets," and in it she described the vulnerability, the risk-taking of putting one's own story-telling process in view of strangers, of being turned inside out this way. She told how the writers of the television show worked together, sharing stories from their lives—memories, insights, mistakes—and combining them with other stories, turning them into something new. She describes authorship as a collection of voices, a state of being held captive together until "you begin dreaming each other's dreams."

While she was there in upstate New York, giving the talk, she'd returned to our old place, the house where our apartment had been. The house looked a little derelict, but had been repainted. She was perplexed about where the doors were— whether they had moved since our occupation. She sent me a picture; the mailboxes have been moved from the side of the house to the front. The long stairway that climbed to the screened porch in back had disappeared entirely.

Her questions about the doors felt crucial. All the ways of egress seemed to have shifted; escape has become difficult, return impossible. She wrote:

> I wish I could have talked to you more back then about important things, and even talked about the future together, which we never really did. I think now I knew then that our future wasn't together and it seemed unnecessary and messy and painful to discuss it. But I also think now that sometimes talking can change those things and I wish I had known how.

SEVEN

- 47 -

Running through clothes drying on a line, my grandfather wrote. *I can remember the clean smell.*

It's the scent of cedar that hooks me right back to Wisconsin. My father would put fresh boughs in the fireplace and the scent of ashes disappeared, as if it had never been. I smell cedar and I am back under those trees, running the secret paths with knives in my pockets, heading toward my secret forts.

I was given the run of those woods, in my childhood. If I wasn't fishing, I was in the trees—climbing them, or scrambling beneath them, crawling through the underbrush. There were always paths through those woods, to connect neighbor to neighbor, and there were always forts and hideouts. When my mother was a girl, she and her sisters built Horse Hideout, a maze of interlocking paths all bordered with piles of white rocks, shards of limestone. My favorite part of Horse Hideout was near the top of the slope, a bed-sized stretch of moss. Deep green, soft and velvety. Sometimes I stretched out, there, and gazed up through the trees' branches, into the blue sky, the distant waves in my ears and echoing off the bluff, the moss so cool and so soft against my bare arms.

I never stayed there long; I had my own forts and hideouts to attend. Squirrel Hideout, Fish Hideout, Cave Hideout, Seagull Hideout, Chipmunk Hideout, Fox Hideout, Raccoon Hideout, Snake Hideout. They were not so well-known; in fact, they were secret, difficult to find. Not far from Horse Hideout was a fifteen-foot-tall pile of stones and gravel, forgotten, no doubt the dredgings of some channel. This was Lookout Hideout, which only I could scale, whose identity was known only to me. From it I could not see far, as it was surrounded by tall cedars, but I could look over into a wide tangle of prickly bushes, and in there, deep inside, was Rabbit Hideout.

Rabbit Hideout was the headquarters, the nerve center, and held the secret to all the others. It was actually impossible to see, from Lookout, and almost impossible to reach. There was only one way in—a tight tunnel through the thick branches of the bushes, under a thick, prickly ceiling. In the middle of that treacherous snarl, the roots and branches had somehow grown upward and tangled above, so a small space was created, just large enough for me, nine or ten years old, to sit there completely hidden. I had a desk, in there, which was really only a flat, rectangular wooden box, one long side open. I kept a spare pocketknife in the desk, and a heavy piece of blue beach glass that I used as a paperweight. Under that piece of glass was a folded piece of paper, a very important map that showed the names and locations of all the other hideouts, their number constantly multiplying (finding and naming them was, after all, the point). At the bottom of that map, I know, was this symbol:

Which was the symbol for my name—or merely my secret symbol, for it had no sound, and didn't stand in as a code or placeholder for my usual name; it simply showed that I had found and named the hideouts, and that I had made the map, that I was master of these woods.

In his journal on July 11, 1938, Charles Burchfield writes, "To see, in the upturned face of a child directed toward oneself, a look of complete trust, liking and admiration is to me one of the finest and at the same time most disconcerting experiences."

Four years earlier, he recounts this story: "Saturday afternoon—took Martha, Catherine & Arthur to see 'where I burned a tree down'— . . . The children expected the remains of the tree to be there yet—I found a burnt stump near the spot which I declared must be the one. This little episode had something of the mystical about it. I can hardly describe how it felt. Somewhat of the strange reality of the dream. I had not imagined that this woods would still have the same beauty or romance that it had for me as a boy; but it did . . ."

As soon as my daughters could speak, they began demanding stories of me, stories about myself when I was their age; I complied, and was startled that the majority of the ones that came to me were from Wisconsin, where my family only lived in the summers—a fraction of my boyhood. Perhaps this disparity is due to the fact that I wasn't in school in those months, and had more freedom, due to the woods and the lake. Or perhaps it's that there was so much forgotten, left behind and unfinished for me on that peninsula.

This past August, I took my daughters there; this was only a few weeks, less than a month ago. It gives me so much pleasure to see the lake and the woods through their eyes, to walk with them through the places where all the stories happened, to be there in those stories and times again.

The three of us, each daughter holding one of my hands, set off down the paths, under the trees. It was a gray, blustery day. My sister's black Labrador ran ahead of us, came back to be reassured that we were following, then ran ahead again.

"Tell us a story," my younger daughter said.

"Show us the forts," said my older one. "Show us the hideouts."

None of it, of course, was quite as I remembered; still, it was there. We climbed Lookout—now covered in ten-foot maples, and sumac, and shorter than I expected.

"There," I said, pointing to an expanse of stones. "Rabbit Hideout was there, all under a snarl of prickly bushes."

"Where?"

We descended Lookout, our feet sliding on the gravel, and came out of the shadows, into the clearing. I stood right where the wooden box, where my secret desk had been.

"Someone cleared the bushes away," I said, "but here's where my desk was, where my map was, that showed where all the other forts and hideouts were."

"So we'll never find them?"

"How will we find them?"

"I still know where they are," I said. "Most of them, I remember."

They began to build their own fort, then, dragging branches and resting them atop one another, making a kind of lean-to. As they worked, I told them about the knives I used to carve, the different shapes and uses of those made from cedar and from birch, the fierce little daggers I carved from sumac. Taking out the knife that once belonged to Mr. Zahn, I broke off a piece of cedar and began to demonstrate.

"If you already have a metal knife," my older daughter asked, "why would you make knives out of wood?"

"I don't know," I said. "It doesn't really make sense. That was just what I liked to do."

The black dog lay in a patch of sunlight, watching us, snapping at flies, chewing on a bone. Overhead, the trees' branches leapt and clattered in the wind.

"A skeleton!" the girls cried. "A human skeleton!"

"Is it a human skeleton, Daddy?"

The girls had found the bleached, scattered bones of a deer, shards stretching from the shadows into the sunlight.

"Maybe," I said. "It could be."

Next the girls found the rusted grate of a grill, and built a shelf upon which they lined pieces of bone, special stones. That would be their food, in this wilderness where they lived, where they had to do everything for themselves. They made decisions; they discussed how their lives would be: a hybrid of *The Boxcar Children* and Laura Ingalls Wilder.

I stood to one side, watching and listening for a while before asking, "What will I do?"

"What do you mean? You're not even here."

"Who am I? The father?"

"We don't have a father."

"Really?"

"We're orphans."

I wandered farther away, into the shadows beneath the cedars, still trying to hear what they were saying. After a while, I circled back, convinced them to let me take a picture.

Then the dog dropped the bone in his mouth and suddenly

barked. He shot away dragging his leash through the underbrush, up toward the road.

We ran after him, laughing, spiderwebs in my face; the girls stumbled, shouting to not be left behind.

When we came out of the cedars, onto the road, the dog was close by, tail wagging, being petted by a person, a woman with her back turned to us. Shouting, the girls went around, past me.

The woman stood, shielding her eyes with one hand, and smiled as I approached. It was Mrs. Abel.

She stepped forward, hugged me quickly, and then leaned back to look at my face.

"You came back," I said.

"I wondered when I'd run into you," she said. "It's been so long." She kneeled again, where the girls were keeping a hold on the dog.

"And what are your names?" she said.

I felt shaky, having her so suddenly there, after all this time. I was glad for the distraction, the shield of my girls, who were shouting, introducing themselves. I looked more closely at Mrs. Abel as she answered their questions. Older, yes, her long hair gone white, in a thick braid, but still slim and strong-looking, still in her faded jeans, a man's Oxford shirt with a ragged hem. My shadow fell toward her, the dark shape of my head across the beaded toes of her pale blue moccasins.

"We found a skeleton!" my older daughter said, pulling a bone from the pocket of her dress. "A skeleton of a person in the woods, near Daddy's old fort."

"I believe it," Mrs. Abel said, standing, and then we were all walking, back down the road, the four of us and the dog, toward the driveway to my parents' cabin. The girls were holding her hands as we walked.

"I've known your father a long time," she was saying. "He used to think he was the best swimmer along this whole shore."

"He still is! He tells us."

"How about you girls—do you swim?"

"I'm an Otter, but I could be a Seal."

"I'm in Polar Bear."

"Those are their swimming classes," I said.

"Impressive," Mrs. Abel said. "You'll have to come swim with me, at my house."

"Where's your house?"

"At the end of this road."

The girls looked over at me. "Can we go there? Can we swim?"

"Maybe," I said. "Not right now."

Mrs. Abel swung her arms, gently jerking my girls forward. Her braid slid back and forth across her shoulders, a white rope against her pale blue shirt.

"You're here how long?" she said, glancing sideways at me.

"Two weeks," I said. "Five more days. My wife comes tomorrow—she had to stay behind, to work."

"I hear it's beautiful," she said. "Oregon. And you're still writing."

"Trying to," I said.

We passed the dark opening in the trees where the cow path led up along the bluff, to where Mr. Zahn's house had been. The girls began explaining the path to Mrs. Abel, and she exclaimed with surprise, as if it were unknown to her.

"I've read some of your books," she said. "I could recognize you in them. And that story about the crazy taxidermist—that reminded me a little of Robert, all the animals he made."

"Well, that's pretty old." I felt the weight of Mr. Zahn's knife, heavy in my pocket. "I mean, I wrote that story a long time ago."

"Still," she said. "And I finally got all your letters, as well. They were wonderful to read."

"You never wrote back."

"Well—" She smiled. "It was years late, when I finally got them. But it was nice to be reminded. That all feels like a different life."

Ahead, the Red Cabin flashed gray through the trees. Down by the main cabin, my sister was packing her car, preparing to drive home to Milwaukee. The girls let loose of Mrs. Abel's hands and ran down the driveway, screaming, the black dog bounding at their heels. We watched them go.

"You sent me the second half of the story," I said.

"What?"

"About the girl and the bird, and the forest underwater. You sent it to me."

"Oh, yes," she said. "I'd forgotten all that, the story—but then this spring I found it when I was cleaning out a storage locker."

"But why did you send it?"

She laughed. "Because it reminded me of you, because you mentioned it, in your letter, and that reminded me. It was something my husband sent to me, once. He probably wrote it himself."

"So the girl in the story is you."

"Oh, I don't think so," she said. "It's not so simple—you should know that. It's a story."

The girls began yelling at me, calling for me that my sister was about to leave. My parents stood next to the car, now. My sister slammed the trunk; the dog ran around and around, then leapt into the backseat.

"We'll have time to catch up, later," Mrs. Abel said. "Don't make them wait."

"Later?" I tried not to sound too anxious, too eager.

"I have somewhere else to be, this afternoon, and tonight. In the morning? You can bring your girls by to swim."

With that, she turned and walked away from me.

- 48 -

That afternoon a storm was rising, rows of whitecaps out on the lake. The girls were making cookies, with my mother; my father sat on the couch, eating peanuts and watching the Green Bay Packers preseason report, complaining about the television's reception.

I was searching through the shelves next to the fireplace, looking for a book that I remembered, from when I was young. Next to my head hung the old marshmallow skewers, long and sharp and shiny, their wooden handles all colors, the paint faded and chipped.

"Is it all right"—my mother appeared from the doorway to the kitchen; she was smiling, wearing an apron with a cow on it—"the girls want to eat some of the cookie batter."

"Absolutely," I said.

"They told me you found a human skeleton."

"We did," I said. "Don't tell anyone."

"They believe you," she said, half-scolding me.

"Not really," I said. "They've known me their whole lives."

"And we met an old lady!" my younger daughter shouted from the kitchen. "We're going swimming at her house!"

"Mrs. Abel," I said.

"Claire Abel?" my mother said. "I didn't know she was back. Where has she been, all these years?"

"She didn't say."

"Grambee!" my girls called. "The cookies!"

My mother turned and went to them, and I returned to my search through the books. I pulled out histories of Door County, and the *Berenstain Bears*, and even books I had written, but I could not find the book that I sought, that I remembered from my childhood. What was it called?

It was a book of scary stories, of hauntings, and the one I wanted to read was about a young woman walking a mountain path at dusk. The light was very important, the haziness, the way that she could not be quite certain what she was seeing. Because someone was following her, a shadowy figure, and once night fell it would be impossible to know if he was still following her, or getting closer, or where, exactly, he was. He? That was what was most disturbing about the tale—the young woman, glancing back, could not make out the person's face, could not even be certain that it was a man, or a person. It could have been something else, something other. She even stopped and called out to it, once, twice, and the shadowy figure paused in its pursuit, but did not answer. When she turned, it resumed its pursuit, always keeping this shadowy, perfect distance.

A little later, my father had fallen asleep, a bowl of peanut shells in his lap. My girls came out of the kitchen to tell me that the cookies were almost ready.

"Tell a story," the younger one said. "A story of when you were a boy. A trick story—"

"But you can't get hurt or in trouble!"

"Someone has to get in trouble, but not you."

"At first it looks like it's going to be you, but then someone else gets in trouble!"

Later that night, I read *A Wizard of Earthsea* to my daughters, in the upstairs bedroom of the cabin. I could hear the wind gusting in the trees and the waves pounding the shore.

"What's an otak?" my younger daughter said.

"Some kind of little animal," her sister said. "That's probably their name for squirrel or something."

I finally got them both to quiet down, and I lay between them, listening to the rain against the windows, on the rooftop, the wind in the trees. The knotholes in the ceiling looked like laughing faces, and the sound of the waves echoed off the bluff, above and behind the cabin, making it feel as if we were surrounded by water.

I imagined the white stones on the beach, the raft rising and falling, tethered against the waves. As I drifted off, I thought I heard a piano—Chopin's *Fantasies*, Beethoven's *Pathétique*, talking back to the storm—and I could feel myself out in the waves, could see the flag at the end of the Zimdars' dock, blowing out straight and square, candlelight flickering in the window of Mrs. Abel's cabin.

High in the cedars with the storm coming in, I sit on one branch and hold tight to another. I shiver, thrilled to think that no one knows where I am, hidden up here in the darkness, and then I imagine that there are others in the trees, all around me, all of us oblivious to each other, all believing ourselves to be alone in the storm.

- 49 -

The sun came out, by the late morning of the following day; the storm had cleared and the lake was almost smooth.

My mother looked up at me from where she was folding laundry. "I didn't realize you were so friendly with Claire Abel."

"Well, you know"—I gestured to my daughters, in their swim-suits, as I crammed towels and snacks into a canvas bag—"she mentioned it, she invited them, so now they're obsessed."

I followed the girls out the door, down the stone pathway to the beach, then pointed which direction to go. We hurried along the shoreline.

Mrs. Abel must have heard us coming; she appeared on the beach in front of her cabin, wearing a white robe, a towel in one hand.

"Welcome!" she said, and the girls hugged her, pulled her toward the water, the end of the pier, where two folding chairs waited.

When she untied and dropped the robe, it startled me, for

a moment, that she was wearing a swimsuit—a Speedo racing suit, navy blue, her white braids swinging against the dark fabric.

She dove, and the girls leapt in after her, and then all three of them were shouting at me to join them.

"Can I wait?" I said.

"No!"

I set down the bag and pulled off my shirt; I unbuckled my sandals, then cannonballed in among them. The water was cold, colder than I expected, and I sprinted out, trying to warm myself before I doubled back to the pier. All the while I was trying to convince myself that here I was, here she was, and here were my daughters.

The girls could not stand, the water too deep, so they contrived a game under the pier. They held on to the metal posts and she and I swam back and forth under the water while they tried to touch us with their feet. I gasped, I went under—my shoulder brushed against Mrs. Abel's leg—and surfaced again. The girls' laughter was so loud, echoing, carrying across the water, that my parents must have heard it, all the way up the shoreline.

At last I climbed out, wrapped myself in a towel. I sat on one of the chairs, its woven plastic straps frayed, faded orange. Beneath me, the game went on; the girls splashed my feet through the slats of the pier.

After a moment, Mrs. Abel came up the ladder. The tips of her braids were wet, sharp.

The girls shouted from beside the pier, holding on to the ladder: "You're not allowed to get out! That's not part of the game!"

She turned to face them, pointed to the shallows. "Bring me a black stone," she said. "The smoothest one you can find."

Wrapping a towel around herself, she sat down next to me, both of us facing the lake.

"Where did you go?" I said, after a moment. "I mean, after that summer."

"So many places," she said. "So many misadventures—it seems like a long time ago, that summer. Who even was I? I got married, and I could see how my life would turn out, where it would go, but then none of that happened."

The color of her hair, the tautness of her skin had changed, but her voice sounded exactly the same as it had that summer, so familiar in my ears.

"When I got the story you sent," I said, "I thought it was some kind of sign. I came out here, last winter, to find you, but you weren't here."

"Oh, I was here," she said. "I just wasn't staying in the cabin. Too cold."

Behind us in the shallows, the girls began to squabble, then found some compromise. Sunlight glinted sharply off the water; I leaned forward, found my dark glasses in the canvas bag, put them on.

"Why did you do that?" I said. "I mean, why send me the story, but also the way you hid it, the first part."

"What? When?"

"In Mr. Zahn's house."

"Oh, that!" Mrs. Abel laughed. "I wish I could tell you. It's just so long ago—I must have planned to give you the second part, but then you didn't stay in the house, and I forgot all about it. Right after that, my father became ill, then my mother. So I was tied up with that, until they passed away." She raised her arms from their armrests, then slowly set them down again.

"But why?" I said.

"Why the story?"

"Yes. And why tear it in two?"

"I think I just wanted to surprise you, to leave something happy behind."

"To entertain me?"

"You could think about it that way," she said, "but it was for me, as well."

Turning, she looked back at the girls, who were running up the pier, toward us, each carrying a black stone. She took one in each hand, exclaiming at their beauty, refusing to compare them, then set them both down beneath her chair.

"We're hungry!"

"We're starving!"

"And freezing!"

I wrapped the girls in their towels, distributed the snacks; they stretched out, swaddled at our feet, and began dropping pretzels and goldfish crackers between the planks of the pier. They squinted through, claiming that fish were eating the snacks, then rolled over, looking up at us.

"That's your house?" my older daughter said, pointing.

"Yes."

"Can we go inside?"

"It's pretty empty," Mrs. Abel said. "It's been empty for a long time. Raccoons got into it and lived inside, all winter."

"In your house?"

"Yes."

"Are they still there?"

"No. A man put traps in my house and caught them."

"Where do they live now?"

"The raccoons? I don't know," she said, "but they sure made a mess. It's taking a lot of work to turn it back into a house for people."

"Can we see?"

The girls were already standing, unwinding their towels.

"No," I said.

"Go ahead," Mrs. Abel said. "There's really nothing much there."

They ran from us, shouting, their bare feet slapping the pier. A silence settled, their voices fading behind us. I stretched my legs out straight, kicking an empty cracker box so it almost fell off the pier. The Reeves' motorboat plowed along, dragging an inner tube of shrieking children; seagulls rose from the raft at the boat's approach, settled again.

"Out on the shoal," I said. "I've been wondering about that night, what happened."

"Yes," she said. "You wrote about that, in your letters."

"Or maybe that was just a story, too," I said. "To entertain me."

"Would you be happy," she said, after a moment, "if I said it was?"

"I don't know," I said. "No, probably not."

"I've wondered about that night, too," she said. "It can't be explained so easily. One time"—she paused, squinting across the lake—"I actually went out, again, to where we were that night, where I thought we were."

"You swam there?"

"No; I had a boat." She pointed out toward the middle of the lake; on the horizon, against the blue sky, a colored parachute dragged behind the parasail boat; out by the island, white sails. "With a map," she said, "and a depth detector, but I didn't find anything, if I was even in the right place. If that kind of thing even stays in one place."

"You were gone for days," I said.

"Once I was under there, in those dark rooms, I guess time didn't seem the same. It was like being half-asleep, and so wonderful, drifting in those shadows."

"I never told anyone."

"What could you tell them?"

"Back then, I mean, when you were gone. I didn't tell anyone you were missing."

"It didn't matter," she said. "And it was so wonderful, where I was. More like a feeling than a place. Nothing like that ever happened to me, before or since. When I searched for it, in the boat, I realized that I was actually glad not to find it, relieved that it couldn't be located so easily."

"You said you could breathe," I said, "and that there were other people."

"I *felt* that way," she said. "It's hard to describe the feelings. It wasn't like something in this world. Sometimes I think it was a mistake to return, and I wish I could have stayed there."

The sound of the wind in the trees behind us, the gentle waves slapping at the beach.

"Should we be worried about the girls?" she said, then.

I stood; I felt a sharp premonition. How long had they been gone?

I called their names. There was no answer.

Standing, I ran halfway up the pier, shielding my eyes, and then I saw their pale faces—suddenly framed there next to each other in the window of the cabin. I waved; I gestured for them to return to the beach. Their mouths moved, talking to each other, and then their faces suddenly dropped away, hidden again.

I turned and walked back to the end of the pier, sat down next to Mrs. Abel. I kept expecting to hear the girls' voices, the slap of their bare feet behind us.

"What are they doing?" I said, checking over my shoulder.

Mrs. Abel smiled; she kept looking out across the lake. "Something we can't know," she said.

When the girls finally returned, they were shouting.

"We climbed your ladder!"

"We saw your bed!"

"What were you doing in there?" I said.

"Nothing."

"We're hungry. We're starving!"

They began rummaging through the empty cracker boxes.

"Lunch," I said. "We'll have to go back for lunch."

"Swim, first," they said.

We all leapt back in, resumed our game; a shorter session, but just as loud.

Once we were out, I packed our things. Mrs. Abel walked us back along the pier to the shore.

"We should swim," I said. "Some night."

"Like before?" she said, smiling. "My shoulders aren't the same, but I guess we could see how far we could go."

"I've been trying to remember," I said, "to really remember the way it felt."

"You're still so earnest!" She reached out, touched my shoulder, laughing at me.

I followed my daughters, back along the white stones of the

beach. Halfway to our cabin, I turned and looked back; Mrs. Abel still stood on her pier, watching us go. She waved to me, and I waved back.

That afternoon, my mother drove my girls to an art camp in Fish Creek. I helped my father clear some brush. Mostly what this meant was I chain-sawed branches loose from fallen trees and he stood to one side and pointed at what could be cut next, and talked.

I was wearing a hardhat and visor, thick ear protection, so even while the chainsaw wasn't running it was difficult to hear what he was talking about. One story was about how he worked on a railroad, how he fell through the open hatch of a freight car and cut his chest on a block of ice. Now wearing his broad-brimmed hat against the sun—holding off the melanomas—and a red bandana around his neck, he told me of how his own father was a master at felling trees, how he could lay them down anyplace he wanted. He told me about how his father always wanted my father and his brother to work with him, but actually he did all the work and they just stood to the side and watched, and listened. This reminded me of my father, and my brother and me, the different axes and hatchets that we used to carry through the woods. Now I was doing the work, and my father, after almost a whole life, had returned to standing to one side, watching.

We attempted to dismember an upended tree trunk, down on the shore, tried to knock all the stones held tight in its roots. We didn't make much progress, and to my mind it was not a task that actually needed to be accomplished, but it was a pleasure to work on it with him, to curse and marvel at the impossibility of success.

- 50 -

My wife arrived, around dinnertime, and we were all together again; we began to catch up with each other, to become familiar, to find and fall into a rhythm.

Later, she went to put the girls to bed, to read to them, and I walked out into the darkness, down to the shore, out onto our pier. The lake was calm; I stripped out of my clothes and waded out into the cold, black water.

I sprinted at first, trying to warm up, out past the raft, pausing to look up, into the stars, before easing south, keeping my strokes steady. When I reached Peterson's Point, I stood for a moment in the shallows far from shore and, catching my breath, looked down at the lights of Ephraim. The churches on the hill, the boats in the harbor.

Then I turned and swam back up our shoreline, past the lighted windows of the Glenns' and my Aunt Dee's, past Harbor House and the Reeves' and our own cabin, where my wife was likely finishing the bedtime routine and was about to descend to the living room, to answer a variety of medical questions from my parents.

I swam on, past the Davises', past the Wests'—now owned by someone else—and over the dark, deeper water of the Zimdars' channel. When I was a boy, I swam this stretch so many times during the day, and I'd see lost fishing lures, snagged and broken off, glittering beneath the stones, silver or gold, still bright or tarnished, and I'd dive down and free them, hold them in my hand or hook them into the fabric of my suit as I swam along. I passed over car engines and train wheels used as anchors, for moorings. Over cribs—frames of timber, filled with stone, meant to attract fish—and across the black channels leading through shallows to docks and harbors, to the boats belonging to the rich houses. I knew that topography, the bed of that lake, so that even at night I knew what was beneath me.

Had it changed? Were those things still beneath me? I swam, that night. I didn't stop until I reached Mrs. Abel's cabin, where the windows were dark. On her pier, however, were the two folding chairs we'd sat in, along with a white towel, left behind as if she had dropped it there and would return for it. The gritty, slick stones beneath me felt exactly the same as they always had, standing up to my neck in the cold water at the end of her pier. I remembered how she looked, shining naked for a moment as she stood there, after she climbed the ladder. I remembered exactly how it sounded, the snap as she pulled off her swimming cap, how it collapsed away, a black shadow in her hand.

The night was so silent. I turned a slow circle, still up to my neck in the water, and could see no dark shape breaking the lake's surface. Far away, on the horizon, the green light of a motorboat slid along, too distant to hear.

I swam back and forth in front of Mrs. Abel's pier. Fifty strokes, turning, fifty strokes again. I hoped to intercept her, and as I swam I felt the same as I did in the summer of 1994—anticipation and confusion, some snarled portent, the exhilaration of being in on something truly mysterious and beyond me. It was, in that black water, as if those twenty-odd years had not passed, or as if their passage didn't matter.

In the end, that night, I did not intercept her. I swam and swam, trying to maintain the possibility, the feeling, but finally I grew too tired, and too cold. Slowly, I made my way back to our own pier, where my clothes lay waiting.

- 51 -

From my grandfather's *Hollow Tree: John Reeve built a wooden horse in his grove for his granddaughters. He found a good piece of wood in his woodpile for the body, but couldn't find a proper one for the head. Finally, he found one in the roadside ditch, but it apparently belonged to a farmer who came to the fencerow to observe him. Embarrassed, John said he wanted it for a cutting block. The farmer began to negotiate. Finally John confessed his true purpose. At that, the farmer said quickly, "You should have told me. Take anything you want."*

My younger daughter has blonde hair and my older one is dark, like her mother. They almost never stop talking, and the next morning as they fished they were discussing the farm they would run, the correct ratio of dogs to goats and sheep.

"Keep the poles out straight," I said. "The tip down closer to the water. Like that."

They clutched aging Zebco rod and reel combinations, trailing lures—Mepps silver spinners, size #2—behind us, fluttering eight or ten feet deep. It was late morning, the sun growing brighter, the lake calm, the breeze still cool.

"A little further out," I said to my wife. "It gets shallow, through here."

As a girl, she attended a camp in West Virginia where she shot rifles, swam in a river, and learned the J-stroke, among other techniques. When I paddle a canoe, I switch from side to side, to keep the boat straight; her J-stroke allows her to continually paddle on one side, not to switch and drip water on our daughters sitting in the middle, in the bottom of the canoe, which is why she sits in the back and paddles when the four of us go fishing. I sit in the front, seated backward, so I can see them all, so I can help the girls with their rods.

"I got a bite," my older daughter said.

"It's just the bottom," I said. "Here, let's turn around, head back the other way. I never caught a fish, along this stretch."

Far away, the dark bump of Horseshoe Island, the white limestone bluffs with the black hole of the cave and Eagle Tower faint against the sky.

"But you caught a lot, Daddy?"

"More than anyone," I said.

"More than Grambee, when she was a little girl?"

"Way more."

As we passed the houses, I told stories about the people who used to live in them. How Mrs. West had once asked for the heads of the fish we caught, how she made some kind of soup from their eyes. She had cocktail parties for the adults and sent us children to the beach with raw bacon on strings, to collect crayfish for her to boil; the crayfish would not let go of that bacon, even as we lifted them high out of the water.

"That's the house, Mama," my older daughter said. "Where the raccoons lived in there. That's where the lady lives that we swam with, that we told you about."

"Is she home?" my younger daughter said.

The windows were dark, empty, but that was how they always looked during the daytime. The orange chairs still sat at the end of Mrs. Abel's pier, and the white towel, too, where it had been the night before.

"Doesn't look like it," I said.

And then my older daughter did hook a fish, and the girls' voices rose, and I tried not to capsize the canoe, to help and yet to let her do the work, to work the reel. The fish leapt and splashed, ten feet from the canoe, then dove deep again; finally, we got it close enough, it tired itself out, and it was lifted into the air and swung to me, so I could unhook the lure from its mouth.

"A big one," I said. "I never caught one this big."

"Really. Is she a girl?"

"Is that hurting her?"

I showed the girls the dark stripes along the bass's cheeks; I let them touch the spiky dorsal fin, fold it down with their fingers. I held the fish in the water beside the boat, to be certain that she was all right, and then she was loose again, sliding into the murky depths where we could no longer see her.

"We don't want to eat her?"

"Not this time."

"I'm hungry."

"Can we go to the Bead Bucket later?"

We turned and circled back, past our cabin again, past the Reeves' cabin that is easiest to see from far offshore, even from Eagle Tower, because of its wide green lawn. On one side of the lawn, the Grove, with its swings, hammock, the wooden horse with the real saddle, just visible in the shadows.

"Can we ride it? Once we go in?"

"Of course," I said. "And then we'll have lunch."

- 52 -

It was my father who found the article, in the following day's newspaper. I was drinking coffee and eating a piece of toast when he slid the paper across the table.

The article reported that a group of schoolchildren claimed to have seen a body. Out off the end of the peninsula, in the middle of Death's Door. These children were on the ferry between Northport and Washington Island, and some had binoculars.

At first they thought the body was floating, motionless, and then they believed it was swimming.

The children were part of a tour group, and didn't tell any adults what they'd seen until later in the day, when they were on the island. They hadn't been believed, right away—it had been taken for a made-up story—but eventually the Coast Guard was called.

The boats searched all through Death's Door, even out beyond Rock Island, but no body was found.

———

After breakfast, I set my plate in the sink and stepped into the garden, toward the path through the trees.

"Wait!" my daughters called. "Where are you going? We're coming!"

"No," I said. "I'll be right back. Find Grambee—she has something for you."

The screen door slapped shut behind them; their voices faded.

I crossed through back yards, parking lots, skirted the boundaries of old hideouts. The distant whine of a motorboat, hidden from view, the hush of a breeze in the cedars above.

The door to Mrs. Abel's house was wide open; on the table rested an apple, a ring of keys. Her blue swimsuit hung from the ladder to the loft.

I could see through the window that the orange chairs had blown off the pier, into the shallows, so I went back outside, around the house, down the slope.

The white towel, twisted and dirty, had washed up on the beach. I stepped over it, wading into the shallows. When I lifted the chairs, crayfish scuttled away, backward, claws aloft. I stumbled, almost losing my balance as I splashed back to shore.

Clouds slid loose from the sun, my shadow black against the white stones.

Turning, I carried the chairs to the end of the pier, where I unfolded and set them down as they had been before. The water was clear, and through it I could see the pale lakebed, stretching away from me into depths I could not see through or into.

And then a flash of blue, of red, and faint voices. Down the shoreline, my daughters raced across the white beach, ready to swim.

Acknowledgments

Thanks first and foremost to my household—Ella, Ida, Miki—whose necessity to me is evident within this book; their patience with me allows its very existence. Thanks to Mark Doten, the exactly right editor, who encouraged me to make it wilder, not to tame it. Thanks to past editors who helped with insight and goodwill: Adrienne Brodeur, Harry Kirchner, Lauren Wein. Thanks to Jim Rutman and all at Sterling Lord. Thanks to the estimable Maya West. Thanks to Colleen Plumb for the beautiful cover image. Thanks to other friends, acquaintances and family—especially my Aunt Dee Brestin—for appearing in this book in ways that might surprise them. Deep thanks to Semi Chellas, for generosity then and now; a pleasure to break up with you, twenty years late. Thanks to Charles Burchfield, who died right before I was born; in his stead, thanks to all at the Burchfield-Penney Museum, especially the hugely helpful Kathleen Heyworth. Thanks to the Guggenheim Foundation. Thanks to Sheri Gilbert for pursuing copyright permissions, and to all the editors, agents and functionaries who sometimes freely gave rights and occasionally charged exorbitant fees. Thanks to the Reed College Dean's

Office Stillman-Drake Fund for paying these fees, and (in conjunction with English Department Eddings Funds) for bankrolling extensive isolation tank research. Thanks to Jolie Griffin for scanning the Loch Ness Monster. Thanks to all at Soho Press. Thanks to Ursula, for her advice, example and friendship. Thanks to everyone else I've met so far.

This book is in conversation with many other texts, artifacts, images and songs. Material reproduced, excerpted or referenced within the text is done so by permission, through fair use, or is in the public domain. Texts and images not listed below are the property of the author or of friends who shared them.

IMAGES:

Charles E. Burchfield (1893-1967)
Forest Fire in Moonlight, 1920
watercolor, gouache, and pencil on paper
26 1/4 x 18 3/4 inches
Private Collection

Charles E. Burchfield (1893-1967)
The Night Wind, 1918
watercolor, gouache, and pencil on paper
21 1/2 x 21 7/8 inches
Museum of Modern Art, Gift of A. Conger Goodyear

Peter MacNab photograph of the Loch Ness Monster. First published in: Whyte, Constance. *More Than a Legend: The Story of the Loch Ness Monster.* Hamish Hamilton, 1961.

Jule Eisenbud collection on Ted Serios and thoughtographic photography, Collection 23, Special Collections, University of Maryland, Baltimore County.

David Seymour/Magnum Photos: "Blind boy who lost his arms during the war has learnt to read with his lips." Rome, 1948.

Albert Zahn
Bird Soaring on a Plane; reproduced in *I'll Fly Away*. John Michael Kohler Arts Center, 2003.

LYRICS:

TEXTS:

Brown, J.R. *The Hollow Tree: A Repository for my Acorns*. Manuscript. 1994.

Burchfield, Charles. *Charles Burchfield's Journals: The Poetry of Place* (ed. J. Benjamin Townsend). State University of New York Press, 1992.

Camus, Albert (tr. Philip Toudy). *Notebooks 1935-1942 (Volume 1)*. Ivan R. Dee, 2010.

Harmsworth, Anthony. *The Mysterious Monsters of Loch Ness*. Photo Precision, 1980.

Hemingway, Ernest. *Selected Letters*. Scribner Classics, 1968.

Hemingway, Ernest. *Winner Take Nothing*. Charles Scribner's Sons, 1993.

Le Guin, Ursula. *A Wizard of Earthsea*. Bantam Dell, 1968.

Lewis, C.S. *The Horse and His Boy*. Puffin Books, 1965.

Lewis, C.S. *The Lion, the Witch and the Wardrobe*. Puffin Books, 1959.

Lewis, C.S. *Prince Caspian*. Puffin Books, 1962.

Murray, M.D., Henry A. *Thematic Apperception Test*. Harvard University Press, 1943.

Oehler, Pauline. "The Psychic Photography of Ted Serios." *Fate* magazine, December, 1962, pp. 69-82.

Poe, Edgar Allan. *The Portable Edgar Allan Poe*. Penguin Classics, 2006.

Rilke, Rainer Maria (tr. Charlie Louth). *Letters to a Young Poet*. Penguin Classics, 2013.

Rilke, Rainer Maria (tr. Jane Bannard Greene). *Letters of Rainer Maria Rilke*, 1910-1926. W.W. Norton, 1969.

Shurtleff, Michael. *Audition*. Bantam, 1980.

Warner, Gertrude Chandler. *The Boxcar Children*. Scholastic, 2005.

Wilder, Laura Ingalls. *The Long Winter*. HarperCollins, 2008.

Wittgenstein, Ludwig (tr. G.E.M. Anscombe). *Remarks on Colour*. Wiley-Blackwell, 1991.

Zahn, Albert. *I'll Fly Away*. John Michael Kohler Arts Center, 2003.

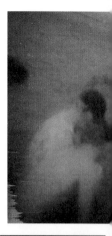